Cornish Pasty Conspiracy

Albert Smith's Culinary Capers Recipe 13

Steve Higgs

Publisher: Steve Higgs

To Susan Cook and Charmayne Beranek for suggesting the title of this book.

Thank you, ladies. I hope you enjoy the story.

Contents

1. Conspirators 1
2. Arriving 14
3. Unexpected Victim 31
4. Chase and Bite! 41
5. The Local Police 46
6. Blood on the Rocks 61
7. More Cops 79
8. Kelly and Liam 87
9. Overwatch 96
10. Conspirators 109
11. Altering One's Appearance 115

12. Identified 135
13. Tanya and the Earl 147
14. Chicken Curry Pasty 154
15. Breaking News 170
16. The Paradox 183
17. Dangerous Waters 199
18. Elevenses 208
19. Who is Following Who? 212
20. Big Sister Power 231
21. A Focal Point 237
22. Loose Lips 249
23. Lies 259
24. Special Mission 274
25. A Plan. Of Sorts. 278
26. Worthless Information 288

27. Tanya 299

28. Spreading the Team 307

29. Out of the Frying Pan 316

30. Busted 325

31. Something in the Water 331

32. Animal Hero 345

33. A New Disguise 364

34. Just Don't Move 371

35. Close the Shop 377

36. Pawn takes Knight 384

37. Stacey and Rex 391

38. In the boat shed 401

39. Gunfire 418

40. Confession 430

41. Out to sea 437

42. Time's Up 440
43. Things Just Get Worse 453
44. Sleight of Hand 460
45. Failing Subterfuge 467
46. Further Out to Sea 475
47. A Sight They'll Never Forget 477
48. A New Clue 492
49. Eyewitness Reports 499
50. Author's note: 509
51. History of the Dish 515
52. Recipe 520
53. Method 522
54. What's next for Rex and Albert? 527
55. Free Books and More 529
56. About the Author 531

Conspirators

"Crazy."

"What?"

"It's crazy, Cody. Insane."

Cody glared across the room at Chris.

"And why is that? Hmmm? Isn't this what you have always talked about? Now we have the chance to do something worthwhile. Leaflets and rousing speeches won't do it Chris. This country needs leadership."

"You're talking about murdering the entire royal family, Cody," Chris replied, doing his best to keep his voice even and calm. He was the brains here, not Cody. Cody was the dumb thug, all bulging biceps and tight t-shirts. No one else had gone to Oxford to read politics. They needed to listen to him. They always had. But now Cody had a ludicrous ... a murderous plan and the others were going along with it.

Flanked by his girlfriend, Raven, the unfairly attractive dark-skinned, black-haired female of the group, Cody openly challenged from across the room.

"Yes, Chris. We do it right or why bother? Are you an anti-royalist, or not?" Cody left the question hanging in the air. Chris could choose to ignore it; it was rhetorical, after all. However, his attention wasn't on the question. It was aimed at the other members in their secret group.

Rodney's silence was predictable and in keeping with his character. He was a follower, and that was why Chris liked him. Together since school, it was through Rodney that Chris met Terry, Cody and Raven.

They all worked together, breaking their backs to make a decent living while the class system in Great Britain did everything it could to keep them under the boot. That he had a degree in politics and worked in a pasty shop served as the staunchest of reminders - his parents were working class, so he would never be allowed to rise to a station more befitting his abilities. Not unless he changed the system.

Chris swung his eyes to look at Terry.

They were in the basement beneath Terry's shop, and it was Terry's business that had brought about the opportunity Cody now wished to exploit. Chris wanted to exploit it too, but not by murdering dozens of people.

Terry was the person Chris thought of as his second in command. Not Cody. Never Cody. Why wasn't Terry jumping to defend his original idea?

Requested by the palace to supply pasties for a royal engagement party – the bride, a commoner, was originally from Cornwall and wanted to bring a taste of home to her guests – Chris had suggested they could bake messages inside the savoury treats. The guests would find them and unable to stop themselves, would read the words and remember them. Chris planned to poison their minds, to sow a seed that would stay with them forever. They were rich, entitled scum and he would make sure the world knew it. The story would break, swiftly becoming a scandal, and the press would hunt him down to ask why he had done it. That was to be his victory, his moment of triumph.

With the cameras rolling, even as the police came for him, Chris Mason would be able to incite the people. They would hear his words, hear the truth of them, and would rise up against the overlords. He would become a legend, uniting the common folk of Great Britain against the royal family, the figurehead for everything that was wrong in the country.

Now Cody wanted to lace the pasties with a slow, tasteless poison. One that would go undetected until it was too late. The muscular moron had even gone to the effort of finding the mushrooms he intended to use. Ones for which there was no cure. Once ingested, the victim was doomed to a slow, agonising death as their internal organs dissolved.

The 'killing in the filling' that's what Cody had called it, thinking his tortured rhyming was somehow clever.

"Well, Chris? What's your answer?" demanded Cody, snapping Chris back to the present like a hypnotist clicking his fingers. "Have you gone soft? You've been talking about this for years."

Now finding he had to fight to bite his tongue, Chris said, "None of you would be here without me."

"That's not an answer," Raven fired back instantly. "We have been offered a unique opportunity, Chris. One you never could have orchestrated no matter what you might claim. All your posturing comes down to this: are you going to strike a blow against the class structure in this country?"

Chris couldn't believe his ears.

Before he could speak, Terry joined in.

"It's a chance to get it right, Chris. We can take out the King, mate. He thinks he sits above us, high up at the top of a class pyramid underpinned by a wealth system that displays his own face."

"He even has people referring to him as 'Your Highness'!" raged Cody, hammering home a point he'd already made twice. "What the heck is that? Or your Majesty, like he glides on a cushion of air or something."

Cody was voicing extracts from a thousand different discussions within the group. Chris had long been a staunch anti-royalist. So long, in fact, that he could not remember a time when he felt any other emotion toward the class system in his country.

The royals were a joke. The late queen's children had made a mockery of the privileges bestowed upon them and her grandchildren had fared little better. None of them were worthy of the titles they held, yet they robbed the nation's treasury to support their extravagant lifestyles and then moaned when they were photographed doing things they shouldn't.

"Yes," Chris nodded thoughtfully to the room as he saw a chance to steer the conversation. "We have an imposter on the throne. He's not even British. Instead of Your Majesty, we should be calling him Mr Windsor. Not that Windsor is his real name. It beggars belief that the nation treasures him as they do when his family changed their name in the war to distract us from the inconvenient fact that they were as German as the enemy. His actual name is Mr Saxe-Coburg-Gotha. It's the most German thing I've ever heard — he might as well be called 'Mr Bratwurst-Kraut-Nazi.'"

There were general mutterings of agreement from the assembled conspirators in the room. Cody, however, wasn't going to be distracted.

With narrowed eyes and an unwilting glare, he pointed out an inconvenient truth, "You still haven't answered the question, Chris. Are you with us or not? Everyone else is on board with this plan."

"That's right," Raven agreed, adding her weight to the demand for Chris to answer.

Chris couldn't take his eyes from her. Raven's relationship with Cody had always been fiery; the couple fought as much as they did anything else. How were they still together? Why couldn't she see that he would be much better for her?

"Chris!" Cody snapped, jerking Chris's eyes upward to meet his opponent's glare.

"All right! All right, dammit!" he snarled, finally letting Cody get under his skin. Exhaling hard, he let his shoulders droop before sucking in a fresh lungful of air to regain his full height. "We can discuss my plan, if that is what the group wants." Chris understood that it was senseless fighting them all at once. He needed to wrap up the meeting and get Terry to one side. He could talk Terry around … away from Cody's insane idea. Then, together, they would work on the others. Or he would be forced to expel Cody from the team. It was that simple.

To begin sowing doubt into their minds, Chris argued, "We talked about bringing them down, not killing them. There will be children at the wedding."

"Royal children," Cody spat. "Every bit as over-privileged and unworthy as the generations before them.

A hammering sound echoed through the old building. Standing on the corner of Castle Street and Fore Street for more than three hundred years, the pasty shop's location on the main pedestrian thoroughfare guaranteed a strong passing trade.

"Police. Open up."

The conspirators looked at each other with accusing eyes. Someone had blabbed. Someone had gone to the police.

"It was you!" Cody aimed an accusing finger at Chris, his lips pulled back in a leer that revealed his teeth.

Arriving

Albert awoke with a jolt. The car had stopped, and blinking into the darkness outside, he asked, "Are we ... is this Looe?"

Jessica stretched in the driver's seat, pushing out with her fingers interlinked and her head down to free off the knot that had formed in her back at some point in the last hour.

Without looking up, she said, "Yes. According to Satnav and the road signs, anyway." Lifting her head, she grabbed for the doorhandle. The temperature dropped fifteen degrees when the air outside rushed in, scaring away the warmth her car supplied.

Albert hooked his coat from where it rested, folded neatly on the carpet under his knees and twisting in his seat said, "Stay there, Rex. I'll let you out the back."

Albert's concern that the dog might choose to dive through the gap to leave via one of the front doors was not unfounded.

Licking his snout, Rex lowered his rear end to the back seat once more and watched as his human clambered slowly from the car.

He sniffed the air, lifting his nose to gather information from the cool breeze blowing through the open doors.

They were at the coast. Even inside the car he'd picked up the distinctive tang of the ocean many miles ago. Filtering out the salt-laden air to discern what else the breeze could tell him, Rex found food smells coming from overloaded rubbish bins, a heavy scent of fish where they were parked next to the market and the quayside. There were dog smells too where stationary objects had been marked.

His observations ended abruptly when Albert opened the passenger side rear door. Bounding out, he stopped just as sharply when his human caught hold of his collar.

"No disappearing tricks, please," Albert requested, fishing Rex's lead from a coat pocket.

Now free of the car, Albert looked around to get his bearings. Not that he had ever visited the small Cornish town of Looe before and would recognise the landmarks. However, he was here on a mission of sorts and had performed some preliminary research.

The streets of Looe were, like many old towns around Britain, too small to fit cars, so Jessica was parked at the head of Fore Street. Behind them, a bridge crossed the river inlet that cut the town in two, and ahead was the older, tourist part of town with the shops, pubs, and restaurants.

Albert knew that Fore Street bisected this part of town, leading from the bridge where the business district started, to the beach where it terminated. To his right was the river and the quayside, the breeze creating sound as it jostled the boats moored there. To his left were shops selling cream teas, cakes, confectionary, and tourist rubbish no one ever truly wanted, yet felt obligated to buy as if it wasn't a real trip to the seaside if one failed to return without something useless and ugly.

To his left, a ten-foot-high poster proclaimed that one and all were welcome to Looe's twenty-seventh annual pasty and cider festival. It portrayed a glistening pint glass of cold, amber liquid next to a plate stacked high with delicious Cornish pasties.

Albert's stomach rumbled its emptiness.

The poster covered the upstairs windows of the first businesses in a row that continued as far as he could see along the narrow street. The streetlights were on, and he could hear music coming from somewhere – a pub, he surmised, glad that he'd been able to reach his destination in time for some supper.

On that note, he turned to Jessica, "Thank you for driving me all this way. You really didn't have to."

Jessica met his honest expression with a slightly embarrassed one.

"And you didn't have to be so generous about how badly I deceived you. You really came through for me, Albert." She fell silent when he shook his head, wordlessly asking her to stop. They had already covered this more than once in the car. "And you gave me quite the story," she added brightly, glad to change the subject.

"Ah. Yes," It was Albert's turn to look embarrassed.

Jessica had deceived him, failing to reveal that she was an investigative journalist who was using him as a distraction to get to the truth. It almost got them both killed. However, he hadn't exactly been honest with her either.

They were even. That was the agreement they had come to, but Albert's story was one she wanted to explore.

On the run from the police, Albert was suspected of involvement in terrorist activities. It was all utter garbage, which the police would figure out if they ever bothered to listen to his story. He could have turned himself in, but he believed he had one chance to catch the people behind a spate of crimes he'd been tracking.

If he did that … if he was able to expose the truth, he would be able to help the people he believed to be held against their will. The police would have to listen if he was able to obtain irrefutable proof and it would clear his name at the same time.

It was a plan loaded to the gunnels with risk, but he'd chosen to do it anyway.

During their nearly three-hour drive, Albert had explained the history of his investigation, the events that had led to it, and his belief in a master criminal operating somewhere in the shadows, orchestrating the crimes Albert had seen perpetrated by hired thugs. Agents. That was the term he'd used to mentally label them. They were agents of the Gastrothief.

Albert could not help wondering if the police might have taken him more seriously if he had thought up a better name, but it was done now.

"You will stay in touch, won't you, Albert?" Jessica asked, not voicing how concerned she was for the old man's safety.

As a retired senior police officer, Albert had a natural inclination to not trust journalists. However, he recognised the merits in having someone with media influence in his corner.

The humans were talking, and it wasn't about anything Rex was interested in. He'd been asleep in the car for the whole trip and now that he was awake wanted nothing more than to stretch his legs.

Tugging at the lead to get the message across, he twisted around to look up at his human.

When Albert failed to react, Rex barked, the loud noise cutting through the quiet night air.

"Hey! It's walkies time!"

"I really ought to let you go," Albert remarked to Jessica. "It will be close to midnight by the time you get home."

"After it, probably," Jessica agreed with a yawn she had to fight to suppress. Closing the gap between them, she gave Albert a quick hug. "Take care of yourself, you hear me? You don't have to risk your life. If these people are as dangerous as you say they are, find them and call the police."

Albert gave her a nod of acceptance as he said, "That is precisely what I intend to do."

He waited until Jessica's taillights vanished from sight, then hoisted his backpack over his shoulders, picked up his small, blue suitcase, and let Rex lead him into town.

He had a rough idea where he was going. Or rather, where it was he needed to go. His accommodation for the night was a small bed and breakfast place in the centre of the town's tourist area. Between the busy businesses, narrow streets of old houses nestled. Protected from the worst of the weather by the buildings around them, many now provided rooms for travellers instead of homes for the owners: it was simply more lucrative to operate that way.

Noting several appealing public houses offering food as he negotiated the town's backstreets, Albert found the place he wanted on his first try.

"Roy Hope?" questioned the man who answered the door. "Come in, come in." Beckoning for Albert to come into the warm, Joseph Hobbs backed into the house down an entrance hallway too narrow to allow paintings on the walls. "I'm Joseph," he spoke over his shoulder. "Thank you for letting me know you would be late. I might have gone to bed otherwise assuming you were not going to show."

Rex led Albert into the house, sniffing in the smells he found and cataloguing them as he went. The house had mice; he could smell their droppings, and the man ahead of him had eaten tomato soup in the last few hours – it smelled strongly enough Rex guessed there must be some spilt on the man's clothing.

"Yes," said Albert. "Sorry to have kept you up. I could really do with something to eat, so we'll be heading back out again."

At the mention of food, Rex wagged his tail.

Joseph had reached the stairs and was heading up them. Like everything else in the tiny seaside house, built to last rather than for comfort, the stairs were narrow.

Joseph, however, was not. A shade under six feet tall, he was as round as he was tall, tapering at the top and bottom like two triangles mounted base to base. Easily seventy years old, Albert's host climbed the stairs with surprising agility and once at the top vanished from sight around the wall.

"This is your room," Albert heard Joseph's voice echo in the quiet house.

"I think you'll find it has everything you need."

Albert arrived on the landing to find Joseph standing beside an open door. Light shone out from within.

It was more spacious than he expected and had a sink and mirror in one corner – handy for cleaning one's teeth before bed.

"Here are your keys," announced Joseph with a rattle. "This is for the room and this 'un for the front door. Mind you lock it when you come in, please. It will be locked from ten o'clock sharp. Now, if you are thinking about getting something to eat, you'll want to hurry. Places are not apt to stay open at this time of year. Your best bet is the Admiral's Knob on Fore Street."

Albert nodded. He'd spotted it on his way through the town.

"They serve a mean steak and kidney pie. That would be my choice." Shooting his cuff to check the time, Joseph reiterated his point about getting a move on.

Heeding Joseph's advice, Albert wasted no time in dropping off his belongings.

Rex understood enough about what was being said to know they were on their way to get food and had sufficient experience in such events with his human that he also knew to expect the ambience and opportunities a public house would provide.

Letting himself out while his host returned to the cottage's living room and the television, Albert paused in the street outside.

On the opposite side of the street at a slight diagonal sat a small hotel. Formed of a larger building repurposed from whatever it had been once long ago in the past, it was the reason Albert had chosen the location of his own lodgings.

If he was correct, agents of the Gastrothief were staying there right now.

Unexpected Victim

Albert's assumption regarding the whereabouts of the Gastrothief's agents was based on evidence. In a struggle at the house of a wine connoisseur in Kent, Albert had come into the possession of a phone. It belonged to Baldwin, a man Albert knew to be working for the master criminal behind it all.

The phone showed a hotel reservation for tonight. They were planning to be here for the festival it seemed and that was entirely in keeping with Albert's experience. They would be targeting someone who was worthy – a competition winner most likely.

Would it be pasties though or cider? Or both? How many people were they set to kidnap and what about equipment and products? The almost undetectable trail Albert stumbled across was littered with all three things going missing.

Catching them in the act would be like finding the proverbial needle in a haystack were it not for the fact … Albert corrected himself … hope that he knew where they were going to be. If they were here, and he wholeheartedly believed they were, then he just needed to identify them.

Would it be Tanya?

Baldwin's female companion, for Albert had seen them together several times in different locations, might be here and that brought with it an additional level of complexity and risk.

Why?

Because she knew who Albert was, would recognise him on sight, and would very possibly just shoot him. She carried a gun, Albert knew that much, and she'd found his house. That she and Baldwin had probably intended to kidnap him was never far from Albert's thoughts.

Leaving the hotel behind, lest he be caught staring at it if Tanya walked out, Albert resolved to disguise himself as best he could. It was a ruse he'd employed in Keswick, posing as a food health safety official. He'd played the role quite convincingly he felt.

That was for tomorrow though. Right now, he needed to get some food.

Rex's nose was working on autopilot, sucking in whatever there was to smell, but nothing reaching his olfactory system triggered any alarms. Recently there had been much excitement – chasing, almost getting blown up, being shot up, getting tasered. Rex didn't have names for many of the things that had happened, but his senses were on a higher state of alert than they might otherwise be.

It was why he reacted as he did.

Heading back toward the busier part of town, the cobbled streets, worn smooth by centuries of foot traffic, were dark and shadowy. But Albert felt no fear for being out at night by himself.

He wasn't by himself, that was the point, and Rex was more dangerous than anyone they might come across.

However, when a dark figure stepped out of a doorway mere feet ahead of him, trying to light a cigarette and paying no attention, Albert was afforded no time to react.

In the half second that followed, Albert tried to halt his forward momentum and saw the surprised face of a young man, his eyes wide with shock, as the two of them collided.

Bumping chest to chest, Albert reeled, felt a hand inside his coat and with a surge of realisation, knew that the encounter was no accident at all.

Rex had sniffed the hidden fellow out fifty yards and a full minute earlier. However, a human lurking in a dark spot meant nothing to him. From police dog training he knew to identify different scents: firearms, drugs, cash. Bored young men smoking cigarettes were not on the list.

Only when the man moved did Rex take an interest and by then it was already too late.

Snatching for the man's wrist when he felt his wallet being lifted, Albert missed. The youth – Albert adjusted his assessment of the kid's age to somewhere in his late teens – was already pulling away.

"Hey!" Albert lunged, trying to grab a sleeve, his collar ... anything, and in so doing slipped on the smooth cobbles.

Rex, unsure what was happening, wanted to intervene, which for him meant biting something until he was told to let go. Tethered to Albert's left hand, his own darting lunge to stop the unknown stranger just added to Albert's imbalance.

As the pickpocket stole a yard, twisted to face the other way, and started running, Albert got a good look at his face: he was grinning and in his hand was Albert's wallet.

Unable to arrest his fall, Albert crashed to the hard ground. Landing face down, the impact drove the air from his lungs, but not to the extent that he was unable to issue a command.

"Rex! Sic him!"

Rex needed no time to consider the instruction.

By the time Albert dropped his lead, Rex's back legs were already driving off the ground, powering him forward to chase the skinny young man. His ears were up, and he was all but smiling at the unexpected game of chase and bite.

Wincing, Albert manoeuvred his hands around, placing them flat on the cobbles so he could lever himself upright. He'd hit his chin when he fell and could taste blood. Using his tongue, he checked his teeth to be sure none were loose.

A pickpocket. Angry thoughts reverberated inside Albert's head. He'd never mocked people who had their pockets picked, but had always felt they had been a little weak in allowing it to happen. Protecting oneself from such characters required little more than some conscious preparation in his opinion.

Now he was the victim and feeling very much chagrined from his position on the ground.

The kid had set off like an Olympic sprinter, vanishing around a corner a moment after relieving Albert of his possessions. He wasn't going to get far though because no matter how fast he went, Rex was a jolly sight faster.

So it surprised Albert when no cries of distress met his ears – they usually followed when Rex gave chase.

Just in the act of picking himself up, the sound of yet more running feet; these ones heading toward him, pulled Albert's head and eyes around in time to see two uniformed officers approaching.

Closing his eyes, Albert tried not to groan.

Chase and Bite!

Hurtling after his quarry, Rex's ears were up, and his tongue lolled from the left side of his mouth, flapping in the breeze his passage created. This was the best part of being a dog – chasing humans to demonstrate how poorly constructed they all are.

Sure, they have thumbs and can operate clever things they have made specifically to employ their odd-looking paws. So far as Rex, and to his knowledge all other dogs, were concerned, there was little to gain by having thumbs and walking upright. It was probably how their sense of smell became so feeble. Up high in the sky, human noses were so far from the source of any scent, they couldn't hope to dissect and decipher it.

The thumbs were good for opening cans of dog food, but such an advantage could easily be made redundant by simply not putting the food in a can in the first place. Humans were unfathomable.

Rounding the corner a scant three yards behind his target, Rex knew he would catch him with just two more bounds.

Something bounced off the top of his snout. It startled him, but not to the extent that he slowed his pace.

Though Rex didn't know it, the pickpocket had chosen to launch Albert's wallet at the dog's head in a desperate attempt to scare him off.

It didn't work, but in the heartbeat before Rex sunk his teeth into the youth's skinny backside, the kid ducked left into a gap between two houses and yanked a wrought iron gate shut behind him. The latch caught, securing the barrier in place though it was almost shaken free when Rex collided with it a moment later.

Rex was incensed. Insulted even.

"Get back out here!" he barked furiously, the noise he made filling the street and waking several nearby children much to their parents' disgruntlement. "This is not how the game is played!" Rex snarled and raged, but his comments fell on deaf ears.

The pickpocket, cash from Albert's wallet tucked safely in his jeans, hadn't so much as paused when he shut the gate. Leaping a series of garden walls, he arrived on Lower Chapel Street. Landing with two feet, he straightened his jacket and hood and then walked away casually, acting like a person without a care in the world.

Rex accepted the futility of his demands long before he stopped barking; he wanted to continue the game. It was only when a poorly aimed slipper flew by his head accompanied by an instruction that fell a good deal south of being a polite request that Rex gave up.

The pickpocket wasn't coming back and the human wailing obscenities from an upper story window had withdrawn their head to go in search of more ammunition.

Rex turned away from the gate with bitter disappointment clouding his emotions. Heading back to find his human, since the old man hadn't followed as Rex expected he might, he paused to collect the wallet.

There was no mistaking that it belonged to his human – it stank of him.

The Local Police

"Are you all right, Sir?" asked Superintendent Charters, helping the old man onto his feet. "Are you hurt?" Heading back to her car, she had heard when Albert shouted at the pickpocket. There was no way for her to know what had happened, but the cry sounded like one of alarm, and that was enough to get her feet moving.

Albert, not needing any help, and wishing it could be anyone but the police who discovered him, made sure to show that he was able to rise to his feet without the need for assistance.

"I'm fine, thank you," he dusted himself off and tried not to show too much of his face. There were two officers, both female, a superintendent, which Albert thought a little odd, and a sergeant. Both were in uniform. "I, ah …" he questioned what he should tell them. If he revealed that he'd had his pocket picked, they would take great interest, ask him questions, request he make a statement, and in doing so would discover who he was and arrest him.

It was the worst possible scenario he could come up with.

"Sorry, I was just on my way to get some dinner, but I stumbled in the dark and lost my footing," he ventured, hoping his lie would sound convincing.

Superintendent Charters frowned a little and blinked.

"I heard what sounded like a cry of alarm." It wasn't posed as a question although Albert knew it was one.

Using the same shadow the pickpocket chose to hide in, Albert hoped his features were less memorable when he amended his previous lie.

"Yes," he tried a smile. "My dog, you see. He saw … a cat." Albert had been about to say squirrel but there wasn't a tree in sight. "Yes, a cat," he latched onto his new fabrication and began to embellish. "It ran out from under," he almost said car, but caught himself before he could for there were no cars anywhere in this part of the town, "bush," he finished weakly, looking around forlornly for there were no bushes in sight either.

"I see," said the superintendent, sounding less than convinced.

"Big German Shepherd, is it?" asked the sergeant. Albert cast his gaze in her direction for the first time and had to hide an involuntary spasm of shock. The 'lady' cop had a head like a bulldog and a body to match. Where the superintendent was lean and tall with the figure of an endurance athlete, her sergeant looked like she could smash through a wall. With her face. And then eat it.

Trying to stop his eyes from flaring, Albert looked down at the ground again.

"Um, yes. He ran off. I should, um, I should ... sorry, how did you know what sort of dog he is?" Thinking too hard on the likelihood he was about to get busted, it had taken Albert's brain a second to spot the incongruity.

Sergeant Andrews nodded her head down the street in the direction Rex had gone.

"Because he's right there," she pointed out.

Rex was indeed in sight when Albert looked, the dog silently padding back along the road carrying something in his mouth.

Sergeant Andrews moved to intercept him.

Rex hadn't heard his human conversing with other people until he came back into the street where he left the old man. They were police officers which put Rex's mind at rest. A former police dog, he always felt at home around the boys, or in this case, girls in blue and had no understanding of Albert's current position as a wanted man.

"Hello." He gave a wag of his tail when one of the officers stepped into his path.

"What a nice, strong doggy you are," cooed Sergeant Andrews. Over her shoulder as she ruffled the thick fur around Rex's neck, she asked, "Does he usually carry a wallet?"

Albert groaned again. Rex hadn't caught the pickpocket, which was a good thing given the circumstances, but had reclaimed his wallet which was excellent news. Unfortunately, it also required some explanation.

"Thank you," said Sergeant Andrews, gripping the edge of the wallet where it poked out from between Rex's teeth.

Rex glanced at his human, checking to see what the old man wanted him to do. Getting no kind of steer from him, Rex opened his mouth and lowered his back end off the cobbles, the canine equivalent of a shrug.

Albert exhaled an exasperated breath.

"Albert Smith," the sergeant read, turning the driver's licence she found so it caught enough of the dim streetlight to be visible. "You're a long way from home, Mr Smith."

It was a casual observation, yet laced with the invitation to explain what the police officers were seeing.

On another person this might have worked, causing them to spill all their secrets like a bucket with a hole. However, Albert was anything but new to this game. He changed tack on them.

"It's a little unusual to find a superintendent out on the streets," he held the senior officer's gaze and continued, "I should know. I used to be one." Albert got to see eyebrows dance. They hadn't expected his revelation. "My eldest son is one now for that matter, but I'm sure I don't have to tell you how frequently family lines run through the service," he forced a chuckle. "So what could it be that has such a senior officer in the field this late in the day?"

Albert knew the woman he addressed could easily choose to not answer, opting instead to fire questions back at him. He'd given them no reason to though, and it was clear they hadn't figured out who he was yet. Were the sergeant to run his name through a computer, it would set off alarms, but why would she do that? He was an old man out walking his dog.

Thankfully, the superintendent felt like talking.

"Actually, Mr Smith, I'm not in the field. Or rather, I hadn't intended to be. I was here on a routine visit, making sure the additional officers I assigned for the festival starting tomorrow were set up and ready. Sergeant Andrews was just walking me back to my car when she received a report of a suspected burglary at one of the businesses on Fore Street."

Albert allowed his eyebrows to rise. Could it be the work of the Gastrothief's agents? If he had it right, then they were already here.

"A pasty shop? he enquired, trying not to sound too interested. He must have passed ten pasty shops as he walked through the town.

Superintendent Charters pointed her feet in the direction of Fore Street. "You said you were heading out for some dinner ..." It was an invitation to walk and talk.

Albert collected his wallet when Sergeant Andrews held it out and stooped to get the end of Rex's lead.

"Good guess, Mr Smith. It was a pasty shop. However, the call turned out to be nothing more than a false alarm. I'm sure that's one element of policing you don't miss. The wasted effort, I mean."

"Indeed," Albert replied so he had something to say and to hide his disappointment. He dearly wanted to ask which pasty shop it might have been. A false alarm might have been someone reporting the sight of suspicious characters where they ought not to be. They would be gone by the time the police arrived, but could easily be the Gastrothief's agents casing the joint.

"Did you have a dinner destination in mind?" the superintendent asked, being friendly, Albert knew, rather than genuinely interested. Before he could answer, she continued to say, "I ask because you said you were here on vacation, and I wouldn't want you to miss out on the steak and kidney pie at the Admiral's Knob. It's quite a gem if you are partial to such things."

It was the second recommendation for the same meal in the last half hour and that was good enough for Albert.

The Admiral's Knob was dead ahead of them, light and noise spilling out from inside as they drew near.

"Well, goodnight, Mr Smith. I trust you will enjoy your visit to Cornwall."

Sergeant Andrews was already five yards ahead of them, making her way back to the carpark no doubt. However, as Albert exchanged pleasantries with the superintendent and thanked her once more for diligently coming to check on him, he saw the sergeant pause in front of a pasty shop.

It was dark – no life from within, but the way she looked at it, up and down and with a thoughtful expression, left Albert certain she was looking at the property someone reported to be getting burgled.

Had it been a false alarm?

He waved the officers away, making out that he was heading into the pub only to hover in the doorway and reverse out again the moment they were out of sight.

Confused, Rex asked, “What about the pub? I thought we were getting food. I’ve had enough disappointment for one night, thank you.”

Albert paid little attention to the noises coming from his dog as he hurried back across the street.

“Terry’s Pasty Shop,” Albert read the sign above the door. It looked quiet enough.

With a festival in the small town, there were more potential targets for the Gastrothief’s agents than Albert could hope to cover. Catching them was going to take some fine detective work. “And a big bag of luck,” Albert murmured to himself.

In the morning, he would get started. For now though, as his stomach audibly complained its emptiness, it was time to eat.

Blood on the Rocks

The sun was still rising when Albert left his bed and breakfast the following morning. Rex needed a walk and even though he had no choice in the matter, Albert was happy to be up and out.

Pressure hung around his shoulders like a lead cloak. He might have evaded the law so far, but he doubted he had long before he ran out of luck. Last night had come far too close, and the relief he felt when Superintendent Charters walked away manifested itself in at least one more gin and tonic than he'd originally planned.

His head was a little fuzzy in the dawn gloom, but the cool air coming ashore with the salty tang of the sea was enough to blow the cobwebs away.

Reaching the last house in line, Albert emerged from the town onto the promenade. The sea stretched away into the distance, curving at the edges where the horizon followed the Earth. The sky above was dark and filled with clouds, but there was no sense that it might rain.

Releasing Rex from his lead, Albert clicked his tongue and shot out an arm – a gesture to let Rex know he could go.

Rex didn't even bother to look at his human. The moment his lead came free, he was running. A slope led down to the sand where he bounded, bouncing like a puppy in his early morning excitement.

A few gulls scattered as he came near them, crying as they soared into the sky. Rex wanted to chase them and jump to see if he could knock them from the sky. He knew better than that though; experience demanded he leave them be for they were too numerous to contend with.

Settling into a steady lope, he meandered across the beach, heading for a rocky outcropping on the southern edge.

A scent stopped him.

Lifting his head, he sniffed the air, testing it and asking questions before setting off again.

Back at the top of the concrete ramp leading down to the beach, Albert watched Rex canter and play. Like so many of the recent stops on his journey around the British Isles, he was not getting to enjoy all that the location had to offer. Given the chance, he would return and do it all again at a more leisurely pace and with distinctly less investigating.

Lost in his thoughts, the unexpected sound of Rex barking snapped him back to reality.

"Rex!" he cupped his hands to his mouth and shouted, though not too loudly. The dog was making altogether too much noise for this time of the morning without Albert adding to it. "Rex, stop barking."

His request had zero impact, and though Albert continued to call to the dog as he closed the distance between them, Rex showed no sign of shutting up. He saw Albert coming though, turning to bark at him before spinning around once more to stare down and bark at whatever had his attention.

"Come on, old man," Rex encouraged. "I know you move slow, even for a human, but you can do better than that. I found a body."

The familiar coppery stench of blood had pulled Rex across the beach to a spot beyond the rocky outcropping. There, beneath a set of iron steps that led from the promenade and over the rocks, was a man.

Rex looked up at the iron staircase and back down at the body where it lay on the jagged, unforgiving stone. That the man had breathed his last was obvious to Rex and though he wanted to get closer, the precarious route to get down to the man was putting him off.

Cursing and muttering, Albert arrived.

"What, Rex? What is it?" He had been about to say something else, but his voice tailed off. Patting Rex on the meaty part of his shoulder, he said, "Well done, boy. Well done."

It took no more than a moment's assessment of the terrain to convince Albert he wasn't going to be able to get down to check on the man's condition. He might be able to go around, but the sensible choice was to call it in.

He didn't want to call the police, really he didn't. Yet again, the likelihood that they would identify and arrest him was going up. What other option did he have though?

Looking around for someone else, hoping they could make the call and he could wander off, he muttered, "Typical," when there was no one in sight in any direction. That wasn't strictly true, of course, Albert could see fishermen setting out from the harbour, but they might as well have been on the moon.

Another person might have walked away, allowing the next hapless dog-walker to find the body, but Albert had preached responsibility his entire life. Today was no time to be making exceptions to his own rules. Plus, what of the man's family? What if on this dreary autumn day no one came along to find the body?

Taking out his phone, Albert dialled three nines and waited for the call to connect.

When it was done, and the police were on their way with an ambulance because Albert couldn't be certain the man was dead, he huffed a deep breath and asked a question, "Who are you?"

That he had fallen from the staircase was probable, though Albert couldn't see how such a thing would happen by accident. Dressed in only a small pair of swimming trunks, the kind people referred to as budgie smugglers nowadays, the man had been on his way for an early morning swim.

Looking around, Albert couldn't see a pile of clothes anywhere.

Knowing it would take the police a few minutes to get to him and wanting to do something more useful than staring at the poor man's body, he set off.

"Come along, Rex," he snapped his fingers and gave the dog a nudge. "Let's see if that nose of yours can find his clothes."

The clothes were not on the promenade; Albert was certain he would be able to see them and expected to spot a small bag or backpack containing the man's belongings. Since there was nothing in sight, he angled his feet in the opposite direction; away from town and along the coast. Setting off over the iron staircase with Rex on his heels, Albert went to explore what was beyond the rocks.

It turned out to be another stretch of beach, and there, tucked behind a rock, was a neatly folded pile of clothes.

Rex had let his nose guide him, sniffing along and alternating from holding his nose high in the air to putting it close to the ground when he thought he had something. It hadn't taken long to detect the ever so human scent.

Snuffling the pile of clothes curiously, Rex jumped half out of his skin when a crab scurried out from under the rock.

“Get back!” the crab warned, lifting his claws in a threat display. Caught by surprise, Rex took a step to his rear.

Unfortunately for Rex, who would have recovered from his initial shock and used a paw to flip the crab out of his way, he placed his right rear paw into nothingness.

What he’d believed to be a shallow rockpool, much like a dozen others Rex’s paws had traipsed through, was in fact the edge of the coast. His paw went through the surface of the water and just kept going. Beneath the gently lapping waves, the rock face dropped thirty feet straight down.

With a strangled howl, Rex fell into the sea.

"Rex?" Albert had been looking at his phone and missed what happened, so it was with a questioning expression that he now looked around for his dog.

Rex was nowhere in sight.

For about a second.

Surging back to the surface, Rex's head popped up with a sputtering gasp. Salty water stung his nostrils and burned at the back of his throat where he'd foolishly tried to snatch a breath before he went under.

"This is not the time for a swim, Rex," Albert frowned, tutting because the dog was soaked now and would take a while to dry. "It's not as if it's exactly warm out."

In that, Albert was wrong, for the sea was about as warm as it ever got. A long hot summer had driven the water temperature up and it was only now beginning to dip again.

Gripping the rocks with his front paws, Rex aimed some choice words directly at the crab who still had his claws up and ready. He was about to start clambering from the water when it erupted next to his head making him jump all over again.

A seal, indigenous to the British coast, popped up right next to his left ear.

"Get out of the water, puppy!" it honked in his ear.

"Yeah! What Gus said!" honked another, appearing on Rex's right side. "This is our stretch of coast. Stay on land, quadruped!"

"Unless you want to go swimming with the fishies," threatened the first, dropping his voice to make it sound more dangerous. "Isn't that right, Robbie?"

"S'right," agreed Gus's partner.

Spurred on by shock and more than happy to comply anyway, Rex regained the shoreline. Refusing to shake himself, he faced back toward the seals to give his reply.

"I fell in. It wasn't by choice." Truthfully, Rex felt like barking obscenities in their faces, but had his sleuthing nose engaged and saw an opportunity to learn something. "There's a body back there," he indicated with his head. "A human.

Did you see what happened to him this morning? The blood is fresh so it couldn't have been very long ago. A few hours at most."

The first seal barked, "A human? What do we care about a human dying?"

"Yeah," agreed his friend, "Good riddance, that's what I say. The less humans the better. Taking all our fish from the sea."

"Yes," Rex persisted, "But did you see anything?"

In response, Rex got a mouthful of seawater when both seals shoved away from the rock and flicked their tails – a human was coming.

"Oh, well done, Rex," Albert remarked, rounding the rock to find the pile of clothing. He wasn't going to touch it; doing so would only mess with the evidence. It might be a terrible accident, but Albert's gut was already listing his discovery as a murder.

Then he noticed the motif on the jacket. The victim's jacket was on the bottom of the pile, but folded so the motif on the chest was visible at the edge.

That the man worked at Terry's Pasty Shop hit Albert like a bolt of lightning. Now he really wanted to rummage through the man's clothes and would have done so had he not already called the police. They were going to be here soon. Too soon for him to start messing with evidence.

Calling for Rex to follow, Albert was heading back to the stairs. It was a high point, and he would be easy to spot there when the authorities arrived.

Rex didn't follow though. Not straight away. He shook as much excess water from his coat as he could, then tentatively sniffed at the pile of clothes.

He could smell the man who'd been wearing them for sure. However, his nose found so much more than that. A trace of grease, the kind one gets from pastry, was on the shoes where the man had stepped in it. Also, the smells of herbs and spices, just a few, which to Rex suggested the man had worked with Cornish pasties. Rex knew the smell of Cornish pasties well enough – his human was rather partial to them.

Mixed in, when he took another sniff and thought about it, was the scent of another human. Another man. His scent was completely individual and separate from the man who'd been wearing the clothes.

What else?

"Rex!"

Rex looked up. His human was calling for him. The old man was at the top of the iron staircase, right above the body and waving to someone unseen on the other side of the rocks.

Rex took a last noseful of scent from the pile of clothing and sifted through it as he made his way back along the coast.

More Cops

Albert had counted off five minutes in his head while they searched for the victim's clothes before returning to the stairs where he knew the police would be able to see him. They arrived a few minutes later, a pair of male officers in uniform hurrying across the town's seafront.

Albert raised a hand to make clear they were looking at the man who placed the call and came down from the stairs and onto the promenade to meet them.

"He's this way," Albert announced, cutting off the introductions he felt sure were coming. The less he said the better, and the body would distract them right enough.

"That's … that's Chris Mason," uttered the first to see the body. "What the heck was he doing?"

"What do you mean?" asked his partner.

"I went to school with Chris. He can't swim."

So far as Albert was concerned that was the end of any doubt. The fact that he couldn't swim and had no reason to be on the beach in swimming trunks when the temperature measured in single digits was enough to convince Albert he was looking at a murder.

The police would figure that out soon enough for themselves, he knew.

Crouching so he could speak quietly, Albert shared his thoughts with Rex.

"This will be the work of the Gastrothief's agents, boy. You can bet on it. Mr Mason here works at a pasty shop. The same pasty shop the cops were called to last night. That's no coincidence, Rex. The only question is whether they killed him by accident when they were trying to kidnap him, or if this was murder because he found out what they were up to somehow."

Rex knew far more human words than he ever let on and was able to understand enough of what Albert said to know they had a case to investigate. His tail wagged at the prospect. There had been a murder. Another one. The old man would do his best to figure out who – Rex watched him flounder around looking for clues often enough to guess what was in Albert's head, so Rex resolved to use his nose to find the killer.

There was the scent of another man on the victim's clothes. It might not be his killer, but it was a jolly good place to start his search.

Extracting the body turned out to be no easy feat and would require climbing equipment to be performed safely, Albert heard. Not that Albert was forced to hang around and watch. Once the constables were on the scene – Albert discovered their names were Lewis and Thorpe – he was permitted to go.

He gave them the name of the place he was staying and the false name he was registered there under – Roy Hope, his old friend and neighbour back home. Roy had booked the place, and Albert knew that if the police came looking for Albert Smith, they would find the landlord confused.

It was better to maintain the pretence and hope he got to move on or was able to expose the whole Gastrothief thing before they recorded his official statement and found out his real name.

Once Albert had used the hairdryer he found in a drawer in his room to turn Rex into a fluffball, he made his way to the dining room where Joseph served a sumptuous breakfast the like of which had only been surpassed by the platter

Edwina placed before him at her house in Eton. That had been only yesterday, Albert had to remind himself.

In the last week he had stayed in … five different locations, he worked out. Five beds in seven days. Were the lives of other seventy-eight-year-olds as frenetic as his? He hoped not and prayed he got to slow down soon.

Mopping up a pool of bright yellow egg yolk with a final piece of sausage, Albert listened for a second to make sure the coast was clear, then lowered the plate so Rex could lick it clean.

Rex made grateful noises as his tongue performed an efficient pre-wash cycle. Not that he was hungry. He'd eaten kibble before they left for his early morning walk, and then chowed pieces of bacon, tomato and fried bread from his human's plate when Albert accepted he wasn't going to get through it all without help.

Dawn had chased away the dark while he was still down at the beach and the day beckoned, but Albert didn't leave the bed and breakfast. Instead of heading out to begin a search for the Gastrothief's target, he returned to his room. There, with Rex stretched out and snoozing in one corner, he placed a small wooden chair by the window and watched.

His knowledge that Tanya and Baldwin were due to be staying in the hotel opposite imbued the hope that he might spot them leaving. Tanya that is, of course, not Baldwin - Baldwin was too badly injured during his last encounter with Rex for him to be here. Did that mean it wouldn't be Tanya either?

The possibility that it might be two people he'd never seen before might have put others off, yet Albert was convinced he would be able to spot the Gastrothief's agents now that he knew what to look for.

Upon spotting them, he knew he would be presented with a choice: follow to see where they went, or head into the hotel to find out who they were.

Squirming slightly to find a comfortable position, Albert watched.

Kelly and Liam

Albert couldn't know it, but his detective work was spot on.

Almost.

Kelly and Liam, two career criminals and former soldiers, were enjoying a leisurely breakfast in the restaurant at their hotel. Unbeknownst to Albert, it wasn't the hotel across the road from his bed and breakfast.

Arriving the previous afternoon, they had already visited one of their targets: an award-winning pasty shop on Fore Street. Earl Bacon had begrudgingly accepted their report that stealing equipment would not be possible without detection in this case. Taking two of the bakers from the shop would be simple enough though.

They could have snatched them last night – the proprietor, who was firmly on their collection list, had been there meeting with some friends in the basement. Grabbing him when he left would have been simple, but not only had the police turned up, forcing a retreat, but they had another target in Looe and both would need to be taken in a coordinated operation.

The Earl wanted a champion cider maker, picking the festival as a venue from where they could select one. For once, the fat, titled member of the gentry had no opinion on whom they were to grab. More often, his own research dictated exactly who was to be taken. They just needed to find a soft, easy target, figure out the best time to take both the pasty people and the cider maker, and they would be on their way.

Obviously, kidnapping one would trigger a reaction. Even if they got away clean, which was far from guaranteed, the clock would be ticking. Someone would spot the first absence sooner or later, so they would find their targets, study their movements, craft a plan to take one then the other in quick succession, and get the heck out of Cornwall.

“What do you think caused the police to knock on their door last night?” asked Liam, expressing a question neither had voiced since they silently withdrew last night. He stood a shade under six feet tall, which made him short in his eyes, a failing he could never correct. He assured himself that it did not give him a complex, but he worked out extra hard to pack on muscle in compensation all the same. His hair had receded in his early twenties, and by twenty-six, he'd begun shaving the rest of it – giving himself the popular Jason Statham look.

Liam was neither happy nor unhappy about being shackled with Kelly. She was rather plain looking, and tedious to spend time with because she had no interest in conversation, but he wasn't looking for a date – he had plenty of attractive women's numbers in his phone.

Kelly, a mousey brunette with a large nose and an untidy fringe that defied taming no matter what her hairdresser tried, shrugged, her eyes never leaving the morning broadsheet she was reading.

"It is of no concern. Focus on the task."

"But," Liam's forehead creased with thought. "What if … what if it's that old man Tanya kept on about."

Kelly rolled her eyes and looked up from the newspaper. "The old man? Really, Liam? Tanya either made him up to cover her own failings, or she exaggerated enormously. What's next? Are you going to tell me it might be the old man's dog leading the chase?"

Liam's frown deepened into a scowl, but the comment on his lips never made it any further because a familiar and unexpected face burst into the room.

Kelly's face registered her surprise.

"Tanya?"

Liam asked, "What the heck are you doing here? This is our snatch."

Tanya aimed a bored eyebrow in his direction.

"I'm not here to steal your thunder, dummy." Turning to Kelly, she explained, "The Earl wants me to catch Albert Smith."

"The old man?" There was no mistaking the disbelief in her tone. "You have got to be kidding me. Anyway, what are you doing here? I thought he lived in Kent."

Now it was Tanya's turn to scowl.

"He knows too much, Kelly. He knows where we are going to be. That's why I'm here. If we are here, then he will be too. I guarantee it."

Kelly made a scoffing noise and went back to her paper.

Liam though, wanted to hear more.

"You said he killed Baldwin. How did he do that? How could an old man do that? Baldwin was in the SAS for crying out loud."

Tanya shrugged. "He got lucky, I guess. I didn't see it," she lied. "The old man's dog ran through my legs before I could do anything to stop it from happening. By the time I got back to my feet, Baldwin was bleeding out. Albert Smith had a friend with him too. I can't tell you who he works for but … well look, the point is that I am here to catch him. If he shows his face, I want you to let me know."

In a bored tone, and without looking up from her paper, Kelly muttered, "Lord save us from decrepit old men and their little pooches."

"I expected better from you, Kelly," Tanya was already on her way back out the dining room door. "The threat is real. Stay alert."

Liam found himself trapped between the desire to know more and the need to play it cool in front of Tanya, a woman whose number he would quite like to add to his list.

As casually as possible, he drained the last of his tea and asked, "Do you know what sort of dog it is?"

Overwatch

Rex was content to nap on the carpet for a while yet grew bored soon enough. Lifting his head, he twisted around to find the old man sitting exactly where he had been the last five times he'd checked.

Rex wanted to go outside. There was a town to explore. His snout twitched as new scents found their way to his nose. Food - that was the dominant smell going around. It had not been absent yesterday, but today was the first day of the festival and the air in Looe was full to the brim with the delicious smell of artisan breads, fatty meats frying, and many other odours too numerous to list.

Rising to his feet, Rex wandered over to give his human a nudge.

Albert glanced down to find Rex's chin pressing down on his right forearm. Reaching across with his left hand, he scratched at the fur around the German Shepherd's neck.

"What say you, Rex? Shall we venture out?"

Rex understood the question right enough, responding by dancing toward the door and spinning on the spot. With an expectant look toward his human when Albert failed to immediately follow, he wagged his tail hard when the old man pushed off the chair arms to get back to his feet.

"Yeah! Let's go find food!" Rex barked, excitement getting the better of him.

Albert checked his pockets, collected the room key from on top of the dresser where he'd placed it and connected Rex to his lead before opening the door.

"Rex, my boy, we need to find someone today." Albert explained on his way down the stairs. "Actually, we might need to find several someones." Despite the obvious clues pointing toward Terry's Pasty Shop, Albert told himself he needed to keep his mind open to other possibilities.

However, in a town filled with additional pasty makers and cider sellers among the many dozens of other hopeful stallholders, picking a likely target for the Gastrothief was much akin to the proverbial needle in a haystack. Albert fervently hoped luck was on his side. If Chris Mason's death was at the hands of the Gastrothief's agents, then the pasty shop had to be their target.

If it wasn't, his chances of catching them in the act were slim.

With that in mind, Albert chose to press on optimistically, leaving their accommodation behind as he emerged with Rex into the street outside.

Had they exited their bed and breakfast sixty seconds earlier, they would have bumped into Tanya. In the space between Albert leaving his window vigil, and arriving downstairs, the Gastrothief's agent had walked down the narrow backstreet and into the hotel he'd been watching.

She'd been playing a hunch, checking the vicinity of the hotel where she and Baldwin had been due to stay. Albert Smith seemed to always be one step behind, but only just. If he was going to show, might he somehow track them to where they were staying?

Rex's nose found her unique scent the moment the front door of the bed and breakfast opened. Like a slap to his brain, insisting it waken from its slumber, Rex was instantly alert.

"What is it, boy?" Albert crouched as far as his hips, knees, and back would allow, getting closer to Rex's head as he tracked the dog's eyes to see where he was looking.

That the dog was emitting a low, rumbling growl told Albert he'd caught a whiff of something. Before owning Rex … actually prior to setting off on his trip around the country, Albert would have scoffed at anyone who suggested a person could interpret a dog's actions and gestures. Now, however, he'd observed Rex often enough to believe the giant German Shepherd was trying to tell him something important.

"She's here," Rex growled, leaning into his collar as he sought out the source of the smell.

A light breeze blew in from the sea, carrying with it a salty tang that interfered with Rex's ability to pinpoint Tanya's location, but the scent was also too weak at that time for him to track it.

He lowered his nose to the ground – he would do it the hard way.

Albert, curious to discover what might have inspired Rex's growling, went with him when his dog began to snuffle along the pavement.

Weaving his head left and right, Rex searched a pattern, trying to find where his target had walked. He might have found it too had Albert not heard the squelch of radio noise heading his way.

That the police would come looking for him to give a statement was inevitable, and best avoided.

Taking a firm grip on Rex's lead, Albert aborted the dog's search, coaxing him back toward a gap between two of the houses. Tucked out of sight, Albert watched Sergeant Andrews go by. There was a young constable with her - a short, thin young man who looked barely old enough to wear the uniform. His cheeks were bright red making Albert question if he'd just been admonished for something.

They passed by without looking his way, and after a two count, Albert slipped out into the street again.

“Come along, Rex,” he whispered just loud enough that the dog would hear.

The swirling breeze delivered Tanya’s scent to Rex’s nose once again when he stepped into the street. Growling, a deep noise emanating from deep within, was shut off when Albert grabbed Rex’s snout.

“Shhh,” he hissed in Rex’s ear.

Rex argued when Albert led him away.

“But she’s here. The woman from … Rex wasn’t sure how to describe the places they had seen her. “The one I chased across the beach in Whitstable,” he remembered the name of the sea-side town where he chased her more than once. “The one who shot me in the butt!” he barked excitedly.

Albert hurried onward, never looking back and wondering if it would be safe to collect his belongings later. Sgt Andrews was there looking for Roy Hope, but she already knew him as Albert Smith. The moment she realised he was one and the same, he would be arrested.

It felt like a net was slowly closing around him. Sooner or later, he was going to get caught and the only question was whether he could catch the Gastrothief's people first.

Reaching Fore Street, Albert took a breath and forced himself to relax.

Ruffling the fur of Rex's neck, Albert came down so one knee was on the ground.

"Sorry about that, old boy. You were onto something then, weren't you?"

Rex licked Albert's chin.

"I wish I could understand you, dog. We need to find two people … probably two people." In previous incidents, the Gastrothief's agents had been in pairs. "Their accents will not be local, though I question how much help that might be given how many tourists there must be in the town right now." Albert was explaining his plan more for his own clarity than for Rex to be able to help. "They will be young, by which I mean thirties most likely, and they will look capable." Albert rose to his feet, groaning a little when his knees protested, and looked around.

In the next twenty seconds eight pairs of people walked by all matching the loose description he'd just given.

Pursing his lips, Albert acknowledged that he might struggle to find the ones he wanted. His rather desperate hope that Tanya might wander out of the hotel opposite this morning had come to nothing, and if the Gastrothief's agents were staying there, he hadn't been able to pick out anyone who fit the bill.

Unable to find them, he had no choice but to head for Terry's Pasty Shop. The body on the beach worked there and that had to mean something. Had the Gastrothief's agents killed him as they tried to get information? Albert knew their MO was to pose as tourists and quiz workers prior to making their move.

But the murder, for Albert was convinced the death was no accident, would bring the police. By singling out Terry's Pasty Shop, Albert was placing himself right in their path.

He was going to get caught.

Blowing out a hard breath just like he was exhaling his negativity, Albert set off to see if his detective's nose would twitch.

Conspirators

In the kitchen beyond the front of house counter in Terry's Pasty Shop, Chris's absence was being discussed.

"You don't think Cody would have done something to him, do you?" asked Rodney, keeping his voice low.

When Chris first raised his concern about Cody's new plan, Rodney had felt immediate relief. It was one thing to want to bring down the monarchy, the joke to the British public that they had become, but another thing entirely to plot to kill them all. However, before he could speak, Rodney spotted the look in

Raven's eyes and had wisely chosen to bite his lip.

Was anyone with Chris or did they all side with Cody? Rodney didn't know. What would have happened if he'd voiced his thoughts last night? Would Terry have questioned whether following Cody was the right thing to do? Rodney regretted not saying anything, but Cody terrified him. If someone else had argued on Chris's side, as Rodney thought they would, he would have spoken up for sure. Then it would have been a split room.

Instead, when the police hammered on the door and broke up the meeting, it had still been Chris against everyone else.

That was why Rodney wanted to sound out Terry now. Surely Terry wasn't really willing to buy into Cody's murderous new scheme? They would all go to jail for the rest of their lives. That was assuming they didn't bring back the death sentence just for them.

Terry shook his head, unwilling to look Rodney in the eye. "Don't be ridiculous, Rodney. Cody wouldn't hurt Chris." Truthfully though, Terry wasn't entirely sure his answer was accurate. Not that he for one moment thought Chris was dead. Rather, he imagined Chris was lying low to nurse a fat lip and a black eye.

Could they do it? Could they really strike right at the heart of the royal family and poison them all? It would take intricate planning to pull it off, but Terry could see a way by which they might come through it without getting caught. They would need a scape goat, someone who would have to die so they couldn't spill the beans afterward.

To give Rodney a better answer and to get off the subject lest Cody catch them discussing it – he demanded they never discuss the conspiracy outside of the group or within earshot of anyone not already in the know – he said, "I expect he's just lying low. The police turning up last night gave him quite a scare."

"You mean Cody scared him," Rodney argued. "For a moment I thought Cody was right and Chris had set us up."

There had been many tense moments following the hammering sound that interrupted their heated discussion the previous evening. Someone had reported hearing voices and seeing lights in the basement beneath Terry's Pasty Shop. Why they might think that would mean the place was being burgled would forever be in question, but the police had come, breaking up the fight before it could start. By the time they left, happy that Terry, the owner of the shop, was there and nothing untoward was occurring, tempers had cooled.

Cody ought to have apologised for accusing Chris – it was clear the police were not there because they knew what the group were planning, but he didn't. Instead, with tension heavy in the air, they'd all gone their separate ways within minutes of the police leaving.

The mood of the group had become dark and mistrustful. It should have been the case that they would be back together and working this morning, but Chris had failed to show at any point. Cody had been in, whistling a happy tune and stealing a kiss from Raven, but he'd taken the van and gone for supplies more than an hour ago and was yet to return.

They needed to clear the air and pull the team together.

This was not the way to do it.

Altering One's Appearance

Walking through the town, Albert passed dozens of stalls. They were set up down the centre of the tight streets so customers could pass them on both sides. Many were selling food, but more had brought art, books, or souvenirs. Roughly half were selling alcohol and even this early in the day, there were people buying it.

Not that all were drinking in the street and much of it was bottled or served in sealed containers to be taken home.

Albert ignored the calls for him to 'Try a drop' or 'Sample the pasty' as he made his way along Fore Street. He knew where he was going and what he needed to achieve. Arriving outside Terry's Pasty Shop, Albert paused to watch.

Thirty yards further down the road, Liam also paused, reaching out to grab Kelly's arm.

"What?" she demanded, pulling her arm free though Liam had already achieved his aim and brought her to a stop.

He pointed, squinting through the ever-moving crowd of people.

"There's an old man with a German Shepherd."

Kelly rolled her eyes again.

"Wow, Liam. Well, we had best abandon our plan then. You do know how much we are being paid, right?"

Unwilling to have his concerns dismissed, Liam persisted. "It looked like him. The old man from the news."

"Oh, shut up, Liam. Or go back to Wales. I don't care which it is, but I'm not going to spend the next two days listening to you twitch every time an old man walks by with a dog."

"I'm telling you I saw him," Liam spat.

Sighing, Kelly huffed, "Fine. Show me."

Liam continued to squint through the crowd.

"He was there a moment ago ..."

Liam couldn't see Albert or Rex now because neither one was in the street. They had moved around to the other side of Terry's Pasty Shop and were now standing in Castle Street. It placed them completely out of sight which was a tactic based on Albert's concern over the police spotting him as much as it was the belief that the Gastrothief's agents might find him before he identified them.

As much as he wanted to go into the pasty shop and ask a couple of innocent questions, Albert chose to approach with caution.

A disguise, that was what he needed.

He'd passed more than one likely looking shop on his way through town, so with a plan to hide in plain sight firmly lodged in his head, Albert retraced his steps.

Rex's nose was working overtime and had been all the way through town. Ordinarily the food smells swamping his brain would make him do that, but today he was doing more with the food scents that just revelling in them. Each grease-laden scent that tickled his nostrils got analysed and compared to the one he found on the dead man's shoes.

He got a lot of close matches, but much like fingerprints, each smell was unique, and it wasn't until he reached the open door of Terry's Pasty Shop that he recorded a direct hit. There were too many overlapping scents for Rex to confirm if the man had been in there or had just stepped in some of the grease outside. Rex would need to go inside to find out.

To his disappointment, the old man started to lead him away again before he could get closer to the source of the smell.

"Where are we going?" Rex wanted to know, his eyebrows pinching together as he stared back at the pasty shop. "I know you can't smell it, but the body we found is associated with that shop somehow."

Rex continued to mutter under his breath until Albert led him into a shop back in Fore Street some thirty yards from the pasty place.

Albert gave brief consideration to reprising his role as a food health inspector. It had worked well last time, but he was in the wrong kind of shop to find the accessories he would need for that outfit.

Stacey's Fancy Dress was a new establishment and one which had ultimately proven to be poorly located. Stacey hadn't done her homework, and was finding that although there was a lot of passing trade and the shops around her did rather well, no one wanted to hire a saucy cop outfit.

Financial worries and her failing business were one thing, but Stacey was far more concerned about her brother, Rodney. She had never liked his friends, most especially Terry, the man who owned the pasty shop where her brother worked. Of course, she'd made the mistake of losing her virginity to Terry South at a party when she was eighteen and had never forgiven him for not calling the next day.

She couldn't tell Rodney that was the reason why she didn't want him to take the job there in the first place, or why she kept trying to convince him to quit. He was too easily led, that was his biggest problem, and whatever it was that they were doing after hours, it had Rodney acting like he had a big, important secret to keep.

They were up to something … involved in something, and no matter how often or by what method she tried to negotiate the subject with her brother, he would not tell her what it was.

Her train of thought derailed when the bell above her door jingled. Stacey opened for the day more than an hour ago and ever since had watched with disappointment as thousands of potential customers went by outside. The old man now making his way through her door was the first of the day to do so.

He had a dog with him, but Stacey wasn't about to kick him out.

"Hello," she waved cheerily, wanting to leap up from her stool by the till but equally not wanting to look too eager. "Is there something special I can help you with today?"

Albert's voice caught in his throat. What was he looking for? He needed a magical outfit that would disguise who he was and allow him to blend in. It couldn't just be new clothes though; both the police and the Gastrothief's agents knew what he looked like. Heck, his face had been on the news, and though it was a poor likeness, and even given the general public's lack of conscious observation, it was still possible the next person to see him might know who he was.

No, he had to disguise his face and that wasn't so easy.

Or was it?

Hastily concocting a lie, Albert pointed to a rail at the back of the shop.

"That. I need that," he announced as he crossed the shop.

Stacey tracked his arm, her eyebrows rising when she saw what the old man was pointing at.

"The sexy nurse outfit?" she tried to confirm, hoping it was going to be a gift for someone who was not the man's granddaughter.

Instead of answering, Albert reached into the rail to grasp the hanger and removed the costume he'd spotted.

"Oh, the clown outfit," Stacey sighed with relief. "Yes, that's most popular," she lied. It had never left the shop, but that was true for almost all her stock.

Grinning and trying to look put upon, Albert embellished his own lie.

“I’m a children’s entertainer. Chuckles the Clown. I’ve been in this business for a good few years I don’t mind revealing,” he made a joke about his age. “But, well, I worry the old marbles are getting a bit loose because I’ve travelled for a kid’s party today and managed to forget to pack my outfit and my makeup.” Looking around the shop, he said, “I’m going to need the full ensemble: clothes, wig, and makeup.”

Hearing the distant sound of an old-style cash register draw springing open in her head, Stacey rubbed her hands together.

“I can certainly help you with that.”

Rex’s right eyebrow twitched skyward in wonder. The old man was standing before a full-length mirror holding a brightly coloured all-in-one outfit against his body.

Conversationally – certainly that was how Albert intended it to sound – he asked, “Do you know if there is anything special about Terry’s Pasty Shop?”

Stacey was across the other side of the shop, taking a makeup box from the shelf behind her sales counter. Returning, she asked, “Special? Well, my brother works there, but that only makes it special to me. What do you mean by special?”

Continuing to act as if it were nothing more than an idle enquiry, Albert tried on a wig and said, “Something that would set them apart from the local competition? Have they won any awards recently? Do they have a famous chef working for them?"

Stacey eyed her customer with a new expression: suspicion. Was he a reporter? There was something familiar about his face, but she couldn't place where she knew him from. He claimed to be a children's entertainer so maybe he'd been the clown at a party she attended twenty years ago. She would have been about the right age then.

The truth was that Terry's Pasty Shop had won an award recently. Well, not an award so much as an honour. A most prestigious one. No one knew about it though. No one was allowed to know. The entire staff had been forced to sign non-disclosure agreements though her idiot brother, Rodney, had told her about it five seconds later.

The whole thing was utterly secret, but there was an old man in her shop buying a clown outfit and asking questions.

Carefully, Stacey said, “Not that I know of.”

Much to her surprise, the old man let it go without a further word on the subject.

“You have somewhere I can change?” Albert enquired. There was nowhere that he could see; people were probably expected to take the outfits home with them, but that wasn’t going to work for him.

Fearing the loss of a sale, Stacey led Albert through to a backroom where she left him and the dog. She was selling him the outfit, but he was bringing it back, nevertheless. She would look after his clothes until he returned – anything for an actual customer.

Ten minutes later, feeling ridiculous, but certain no one was going to spot him for who he really was, Albert inspected his face in the mirror. In a moment of irony, he'd chosen to go with the bald wig to hide his, err … bald head. As a disguise it worked better than he could have hoped. The makeup was as close as he could get to the image in his head; all bright colours around the eyes and mouth.

"Not bad, Albert Smith. Not bad," he congratulated himself on a job well done.

Sure, he looked like a total jerk, but he did not look like Albert Smith.

"Everything fit okay?" Stacey asked upon hearing the old man returning from the back of her shop. Positioning herself behind the sales counter, she turned around to face her customer and screamed.

Rex jumped out of his skin, darting back a yard and barking and Albert came close to needing new pants.

Stacey clung to the counter, catching her breath as her heart jackhammered.

"Woooo. Sorry about that. You caught me by surprise is all."

"Okaaaay," Albert wasn't sure what could possibly have caused her reaction.

"You said you entertain children, right?"

"Yes. Why?"

"Oh, no reason," she lied. Stacey had a thing about clowns; they creeped her out. That was just ordinary clowns though. Ones with happy makeup. Albert's attempt at a traditional clown face left him looking like the only thing he planned to do with the children was eat their kidneys.

Keen to get the terrifying face out of her shop, Stacey rang up the bill.

"Cash?" Albert asked as he rooted around in his trousers to find his wallet. The pickpocket had made off with almost a hundred pounds. It was annoying, but not disastrous. The bulk of Albert's cash had been secure in his suitcase back in his room.

Opening his wallet, Albert looked up to find an apologetic expression plastered across Stacey's face.

"Sorry. This is a cashless business," she replied, eyeing the rows of cards on display.

Albert's fingers were on the cash tucked into a fold at the back. Roy had been good enough to forward him a wad of it, knowing his old friend would return it the first moment he was able. Cash was important because the police would have trackers attached to his cards. The moment he used one, they would know where he was and would come running.

He couldn't afford to let that happen yet, not when he was so close.

With his mind racing, Albert thought about what he could say to politely deny the lady the sale dangling in her face. He never got the chance.

"Albert Smith," Stacey read from the face of Albert's driving license where it sat in a clear plastic slot on the left hand side.

She picked up her phone, but before she could use it, her brain supplied the answer she sought. Her eyes drifted upward to meet Albert's and she knew she had it right.

Identified

"Albert Smith!" she blurted, backing away. "You're the terrorist who blew up the beach in Whitstable!"

"That's not accurate," he tried to defend himself, though his heart wasn't really in it.

The girl looked terrified, which in turn horrified Albert – he'd never wanted to scare anyone.

Stacey had backed away from the man she now recognised from the national news, but there was nowhere for her to go. Inadvertently, she'd trapped herself behind the counter, from which the only way out was through the old man.

"I'm ... I'm calling the police!" she blurted, glancing down to where her phone lay on the counter and calculating whether she could get to it first.

"Of course," Albert nodded, "I won't try to stop you." He hated that it had come to this, but what were his options? Run? He was seventy-eight years old and though some might consider him to be sprightly, he wasn't about to perform an intricate parkour route across the roofs of Looe to evade the law. Plus, he was now dressed as a clown and would be visible from space, so if a manhunt ensued, it would be the shortest in history. Albert could already envisage the years of torment his children would suffer as the blooper reels replayed his arrest around the globe.

Darting forward, one hand ready to fend off her attacker, Stacey was still figuring out what Albert had just said when she grabbed the device. With it in her hand, she didn't even need to call the police, just using the voice recognition software would do it, but the old man wasn't even trying to stop her.

"What's going on?" asked Rex, the dog's curious expression and Albert's attention on it, further softening Stacey's opinion.

The old man had dropped slowly to one knee and was telling the dog that he was going to have to go with the police when they came. He sounded upset and it was throwing her completely.

"What do you mean the news isn't accurate?" she asked, her phone gripped tightly in one hand.

Albert looked up from his position near the floor. There was a tear brimming in the corner of his right eye. Not for himself - he would never stoop to self-pity, but from concern for what might happen to Rex.

"Just that, my dear. I'm investigating a series of crimes and got close enough to the people behind it that the police now believe I am connected to what happened in Whitstable."

"And you are telling me that you are not?"

"Seriously," Rex nudged his human. "What's happening? I'm getting hungry and all the food smells around here are driving me a little bit nuts. I need to get back to the murder investigation to distract myself. I think I can find the person who left their scent on the dead man's clothing."

Albert scratched under Rex's ears, comforting himself as much as the dog.

Responding to Stacey, he said, "I don't expect you to believe me, but I'm completely innocent of all charges. You'll ask me why I haven't turned myself in if that's the case and the simple answer is that I cannot prove my innocence. That's what I am here to do."

Stacey knew the only sensible course of action was to call the police. However, the old man reminded her just a little bit too much of her grandfather. She and Rodney lost him less than a year ago and the memory of his passing still stung.

"Why did you ask about the pasty shop? What do you know about it?"

Noting that the young woman was yet to call for help, and gripping hold of the thin sliver of hope he could perceive, Albert rose from the floor, his arms splayed to show they were empty.

"I don't 'know' anything about it, my dear. Other than I believe it to be the target of the same gang of criminals I have been tracking across the country."

"So you don't know about the royal appointment?" Stacey was more confused than ever now.

Albert needed to explore what that meant, but first chose to test the waters. Now that Stacey knew his secret, maybe he could pick her brain for information.

"Your brother works there. Do you know Chris Mason?"

Stacey blinked. "Chris? Yes, I know him. What about him?"

Albert rolled his lips inward, chewing on them for a second before replying.

"I'm sorry to tell you that he's dead. I think someone killed him last night and that would fit with the pattern I have been following."

Stacey heard the words leaving the old man's mouth, but they got a little jumbled in her head. There was a moment when she felt a little dizzy and the next thing she knew, the old man was crouched over her and the dog was breathing in her left ear, its breath hot and moist.

"Ewww," she scooted away a foot, bumping into Albert's feet. There was a fleeting thought to run screaming from the shop but mercifully her brain caught up with itself first.

"I fainted, didn't I," she asked.

Albert moved back, clicking his tongue at Rex to make him move too.

"I'm afraid so. Are you feeling all right? I'm sorry if I gave you a shock."

"You didn't leave," Stacey remarked. "You could have left me here. You could have tied me up and left me here. No one would have found me for hours."

Albert smiled, hoping it would put her at ease. "That would hardly be in keeping with protesting my innocence. I can leave now if you want me to, but there really won't be any point if you are going to call the police the moment I walk out the door."

Stacey didn't know what to make of the old man. The truth was that she believed him. Nothing about the way he spoke or the way he acted gave her any reason to believe he could be involved in any criminal or terrorist activity. However, it wasn't that which drove her to offer her help.

It was the returning memory of why she fainted.

Her hand shot to her mouth.

"Oh, my God. Chris!" Stacey took out her phone, murmuring to herself, "I need to talk to Rodney. You think someone killed him?"

Albert did his best to make his expression solemn and trustworthy. Unfortunately, with the evil clown make up, his best efforts made Stacey wonder if he'd just found a hedgehog in his jockey shorts.

"I'm afraid so," he replied. "He worked at Terry's Pasty Shop, didn't he?" Albert wanted to be doubly sure he had that right.

"Yes."

"The people I am following, the reason I am here and in so much trouble ... they kill people. If I can identify them, I can stop them." Worried that he might come across as overconfident or perhaps even arrogant, he added, "I hope."

Albert couldn't guess how the fancy dress shopkeeper might respond. Honestly, he was shocked she hadn't called the police, but what she said next was not what he expected.

"I think there's something going on at the pasty shop," she announced out of the blue. "I'm worried my brother might be getting himself into trouble. If I don't turn you in, will you help me to figure out what it is?"

Albert knew he was going to agree to her terms; it wasn't as if he had a choice, but he didn't say 'Yes' he said, "What sort of trouble?"

Tanya and the Earl

Liam and Kelly were scoping out cider makers when Albert left the fancy dress shop right behind them. The earl had given them free rein to pick a cider maker of their choosing. Well, sort of. Whoever they went for needed to be an award winner with the ability to craft multiple flavours from scratch given raw ingredients.

The earl knew making cider was relatively easy, but that was only true when looking at the product from the perspective of making an alcoholic drink from apples. He wanted something vastly more refined than that, so his instruction had been to target craft cider makers. He wanted someone who would produce a drink that was the Earl's and the Earl's alone.

There were too many for them to pick from, but that was okay because there was a contest happening tonight. The festival was to spill onto the beach where live bands would entertain the crowds and the town would revel in the additional income flowing from the visitors' pockets.

The cider makers knew the winner would be the 'guest' beverage in half the pubs and bars in the area by the following day and the winner was to be announced before the headline acts took to the stage.

All Liam and Kelly needed to do today was scope out the various craft brewers and know their locations. They would grab the winner secure in the knowledge that would tick the Earl's boxes. The best time for that would be after the festival ended, but the Earl wasn't inclined to wait.

According to him, the end of the world was too close now. He needed to secure the final elements of his larder before the cataclysm occurred.

Neither Liam nor Kelly gave comment upon hearing his instructions nor bothered to discuss his insanity afterward. He paid well and that was all that mattered. Despite that, both harboured an unspoken curiosity about what the Earl would do when the end of the world didn't occur. He would know the planet continued to spin, its inhabitants going merrily about their lives because he watched the news.

Earl Bacon was getting ready to seal the doors to his underground lair, so the only question was whether he would accept that he had it wrong and opened them again at any point.

It was not a subject they dwelled on for long. They were nearing the end of their contract and would be far away when the outer doors sealed everyone inside.

In contrast to their relaxed attitude toward the impending Armageddon the Earl believed to be approaching, their employer was beside himself with worry.

Impatiently, he waited for the call he'd placed to connect.

"Earl Bacon," Tanya drawled, certain she knew why he was calling and already unhappy about it.

"You're in Cornwall!" he declared. "I explicitly told you to go after Albert Smith. I assigned the Cornish task to Liam and Kelly, yet I learn that you have disobeyed me and gone there anyway, Tanya. Please explain."

Earl Bacon was only willing to give Tanya the opportunity to explain because she had proven to be such a reliable asset in the past. Anyone else would have been forced to listen to a lambasting.

Speaking slowly and doing so deliberately because she knew it would sound like she was talking to an idiot, she said, "I am in Cornwall because Albert Smith is in Cornwall."

The Earl said nothing for several seconds, giving himself time to process the news before he asked, "How do you know that? Kelly gave no indication that she felt the operation was in jeopardy."

So it was Kelly who told the Earl. Tanya had suspected that would be the case. They'd been something close to friends for a short while. Right up until the Earl began to favour Tanya and give her the better assignments. Better in Kelly's eyes anyway.

Dropping the slow speech, Tanya said, "My dear Earl, the only reason you have sent me after Albert Smith is because he keeps showing up to interfere with your operations. Yes, he could show at any one of half a dozen different locations because Kelly's assignment in Cornwall is far from the only one taking place today. However, since I cannot be everywhere, I hedged my bets and went to where Baldwin and I were scheduled to be. If Albert Smith shows his face in Looe, I will kill his dog and bring his battered, unconscious body to you."

Chicken Curry Pasty

Upon agreeing to help Stacey, Albert had learned a surprising secret: Terry's Pasty Shop was supplying the royal family, specifically the engagement party of Prince Marcus. The news was a revelation because Albert wasn't even aware the youngest prince was engaged. Stacey explained that it wasn't public knowledge, and she only knew because her brother is an idiot.

Norma Morley – a name Albert thought he might have heard once or twice in connection with Prince Marcus – wanted a relaxed wedding, not the grand, stately affair the royal family expected. Part of that was the food, which Stacey knew nothing about other than the desire to serve guests some Cornish pasties at the young couple's engagement party. Norma Morley chose ones she remembered from her childhood – those served in Terry's Pasty Shop in the heart of Looe.

Albert thought it a strange tale, but could see no reason to doubt a word of it. That Stacey could give no steer regarding what she thought her brother might be involved in made the whole thing sound far more mysterious than Albert imagined it would prove to be. Nevertheless, her desire to have him poke into the undercurrent of occurrences at Terry's Pasty Shop aligned neatly with his own needs. Not only that, he'd learned more since Stacey 'outed' him than he could have hoped to by himself.

It was the local help angle again and he embraced it as he knew he should.

It was why he agreed to leave Rex with Stacey and was heading for the pasty shop where her brother worked. They were standing together in the street watching him walk away. Albert could tell Rex wasn't happy about it, but it was only temporary.

Stacey made the call to her brother, but with Albert coaching her, tactfully broke the news, and asked whether Chris had been talking or meeting with anyone new?

He hadn't. At least not according to Rodney. Nor did Rodney believe he'd noticed anyone nosing around the shop or asking questions.

Unsure of what to expect, Albert pressed on. Delightfully enticing smells, borne on the air and drifting down the street, had grabbed his nostrils the moment he left Stacey's place.

Halfway to his destination he heard a child say, 'Ooh, look, Mummy! A clown!' he turned to offer her a smile and got to see terror form on the little girl's face. She screamed, burying her face in her mother's coat. He got a scowl from the lady as she hurried away with her sobbing child.

Confused, he checked his reflection in a shop window. Was there something wrong with his makeup?

Unable to figure out what the little girl's problem was, he pushed onward to the shop.

Now staring down at the flaky pastry goodness stacked beneath a glass counter, the pasty smells made a beeline for his stomach. It growled even though he knew he ought not to be hungry.

A small queue leading to the counter meant there was time to look and listen. The dead man at the beach had worked here. The police felt the need to visit here last night following a report of … something. Burglary was what Superintendent Charters said, but also that it was a false alarm.

Was it though? Okay, so it wasn't burglary, but it had to have been something and one of the people who worked here was dead this morning.

Though hope was hardly a tactic, Albert clung to the wish that he might have already found the Gastrothief's target. In an otherwise sleepy seaside village in late autumn, what else could be behind the odd events at this pasty shop?

Out in the street, Rex had watched his human walk away. Glancing up at the woman now holding his lead, he questioned, yet again, what was happening.

The old man had gone back to the pasty shop, and that was in keeping with Rex's expectations. His nose knew for certain that the human scent he found on the dead man's clothes came from there. What made no sense was his human going without him.

Rex's nose was needed and the more he thought about the old man's pathetic sense of smell, the more agitated he became.

Rising to his feet, he decided that it was time to do what he knew to be right.

"Whoa! Where do you think you're going?" Stacey asked, reeling Rex in before he could get going.

Rex shot her a disparaging look. "I'm sure you are a perfectly nice human, but you're not my human and he's the one I care about. Sorry." With that, he threw his body backward to tense his leg muscles and leapt forward, confident he had enough strength to tear the lead from the woman's hands.

He did.

With an expletive aimed at his back, Rex bounded down the street. Weaving between the stalls and the people pressing in around them, he applied the brakes only when he reached the open door to the pasty shop. There, he checked inside but did not go in.

Rex could see his human at the shop's counter. He was talking to a woman on the other side and appeared to be in no danger. Convinced he had a little time to go snooping, Rex made his way around the outside of the shop, snuffling along to let his nose lead the way and, for once, using his eyes.

Finding a gate leading into a yard behind the shop, he nudged it open, and went inside.

In the shop, Albert was doing what he could to extract information without triggering anyone's suspicions.

"I recently visited Biggleswade and ate their famous clanger. Have you ever had one?" he enquired of the raven-haired woman behind the counter.

Raven did her best not to sigh or tut. There was no one queuing behind the old man but that wouldn't last for long, and either way, she had no desire to exchange small talk with him. Rodney and Terry were arguing about something in the kitchen. She couldn't make out enough words to know what had them so stirred up, but had definitely heard them say "Cody and Chris" more than once.

Focussing on the old man dressed as a psycho clown, she gave a dismissive reply, "Never heard of a clanger." Looking down at the array of pasties filling the glass fronted cabinet, she offered, "The steak and stilton pasty is one of our best sellers if you are looking for something a little different. Or the chicken curry pasty is quite popular."

"Chicken curry pasty?" Albert repeated the words with all the disdain he could muster. However it might taste, it sounded like an abomination. The steak and stilton was intriguing, and he chose to get one, but delayed placing his order so he could begin a new line of conversation.

"I wonder, can I ask if you have had anyone come by in the last twenty-four hours asking questions about the business?"

Raven stared across the countertop, her face frozen save for her eyes which blinked twice.

Pressing on, Albert abandoned pretence in favour of expediency, "What I mean to say is that I know this establishment won a coveted honour recently. A very secret contract," he dropped his voice so he was almost whispering. "I fear there may be reason to believe this will attract ... unwanted attention from a third party," Albert selected his words with care. He couldn't introduce the concept of the Gastrothief without sounding insane at the best of times and today he was dressed as Chuckles, the clown who likes to murder people.

There was a commotion taking place in the back room beyond the woman he was talking to, and it was clear to Albert she was finding it distracting. Up until he mentioned the secret thing, that is. Now her eyes were wide, and her mouth hung open.

"How ..." she began to ask, but closed her mouth. With a nervous smile, she said, "One moment, please," and ducked out the back leaving her companion to manage the shop.

Unsure what to do, Albert smiled at the teenager left to man the shop, though he relaxed his facial muscles when he saw a terrified expression filling the girl's face.

At the back of the pasty shop, Rex was peering in through a plastic door flap. Hung to make egress and entry swift when the staff went out to the chillers and storerooms located outside, the sheet of thick plastic was designed to be pushed aside, so that was what Rex had done.

Now with his head inside the kitchen, his nose was filled with the glorious scents coming from a hundred hot pasties fresh from the oven. It was all a bit too much; the hardwired demand to eat fought against his will to investigate and neither was winning. Long drool candles hung from each side of his mouth.

With his eyes closed, he focused on everything apart from the heavenly smell of food.

“Come on, Rex, you can do this,” he chanted inside his head. “You can do this.”

There were humans in the kitchen, just out of sight around a corner. He would be able to see them if he went a few more feet inside, but didn’t want to get caught.

He did want a pasty though, he caught his unconscious mind commenting.

“No! No pasty,” he argued. “Focus on the job, Rex.”

Sniffing deeply again, he found the scent of several different humans. One by one, he compared them to the scent he found on the pile of clothing earlier. Much like matching handwriting, the scent of a woman - a combination of perfumed products, her natural body odour, and the detergent she used on her laundry – made her stand out like a red mark on a white sheet. He dismissed her smell and moved to the next.

He was looking for a man, he already knew that. A specific man.

That man had been in the pasty shop, but was not here now. The same could be said of the dead man, who was, of course, also not here now. That both the victim and the man who left his scent on the victim's clothes appeared to inhabit the same space had to mean something. Rex wasn't sure what that could be.

Yet.

Breaking News

Inside the kitchen the discussion was really heating up.

“What do you mean Chris is dead?” Raven had Rodney by his collars.

“That’s what Stacey told me,” Rodney gibbered. He really wasn’t a fan of confrontation and had no idea what to do about Raven grabbing him. Did he push her away? What if he accidentally caught a handful of boob? She was Cody’s girlfriend and Rodney wasn’t going to mess with him no matter what.

“Stacey?” Raven recoiled. “That idiot sister of yours?”

Rodney tried to defend her, “Well, I’m not sure I would label her as a …”

“Shut up!” Raven snapped. “Just shut your mouth. Chris is not dead. He can’t be.”

Terry attempted to calm things down when he calmly asked, “Then why didn’t he show up for work this morning? Why isn’t he answering his phone?” They were good questions, and everyone had been wondering the same thing. Not only that, they all knew Chris wasn’t on board with Cody’s plan and that Cody had a temper.

Terry’s softly spoken question cooled the temperature a few degrees, taking some of the steam out of Raven's anger. She almost let Rodney go, but chose at the last second to deliver a swift knee between his legs, just because she knew he would do nothing about it.

As he slumped to the kitchen floor, she remembered why she had come into the kitchen in the first place.

"There's an old man out front dressed as a psycho clown and asking about the royal engagement contract."

"What!" Terry spasmed with shock. "No one knows about that! Who is he?"

"How the hell should I know?" Raven snarled in Terry's face.

Rex could hear the argument raging inside but found the words came too fast for him to understand. That didn't bother him because humans lied at least half the time. Their words could be misleading – 'We're just going for a nice walk' had been code for a trip to the vets one time too many, but their smell never lied.

The scent was the truth.

Sneaking further into the kitchen, Rex pushed past the plastic curtain. Pausing at the end of the short corridor that led from the back door, he peered around the corner - there were too many odours in too small a space for his nose to be effective at his current range.

There were three humans in sight; a sniff confirmed they were the only three in the kitchen. The scents of the two men and the woman were completely intermingled, which to Rex meant they had either been mating or fighting. He already knew it was the latter from the raised voices, but the tang of blood he thought he might find on them was absent.

If one of them was responsible for the body at the beach, they had done a good job of removing the smell.

A noise from behind Rex gave him a start: someone was coming! The three humans in the kitchen were still arguing, their attention on each other. With his escape route cut off, Rex did the only thing he could.

Out in the pasty shop's front of business, Albert waited for Raven to return. He knew her name because the teenager left to mind the shop and deal with customers had assured him, 'Raven would return momentarily'. She was serving other customers now, each new person entering the shop shooting a strange look at the frightening clown and opting to give him a wide berth.

Looking through the gap that led into the kitchen for any sign of Raven's return and hoping she was fetching the proprietor, Albert thought, just for a moment, that he saw a dog's tail flitting by in the distance.

Frowning, he glanced back up the road to see if he could spot Stacey and Rex. To his surprise, and accompanied by a lurch from his heart, he saw the police. Stacey was nowhere in sight.

Stacey, unbeknownst to Albert, was hiding around the other side of the shop. Tucked into an alcove on Castle Street, she bit her fingernails and wondered what to do. When the stupid dog snapped the lead from her hands, she gave chase. Not that she believed she could keep up with Rex - it was an instinctive thing to do.

Had Rex not taken the next right turn, and had she not been following as fast as she could, she would not have seen him sneak into the backyard of Terry's Pasty Shop.

Stacey followed him there too, but the dog was nowhere in sight by the time she got through the gate, and she wasn't prepared to waltz into the kitchen, not if it meant she might bump into Terry.

Instead, she retreated from the yard, backing across the narrow street to a place where she could watch the gate and be ready when the people inside chased Rex out. That was what she believed would happen, and it was with horror that she saw Cody arrive.

She knew Cody only by reputation. He was a thug. A bully. Someone to avoid. Watching in horror, Stacey saw him follow where Rex had gone.

"What's happening?" Cody asked, his tone light and curious as he came into the kitchen. He'd snagged his apron on the way in and was already tying it around his waist as he made his way to the sinks to wash his hands.

Rodney was slumped against a wall holding his sides and the tension in the air could be cut with a knife.

Terry answered before Raven could. “Rodney’s sister says Chris’s body was found on the beach this morning.” It wasn’t a direct accusation, but it came close. Of all the members of their group, Terry was the one least intimidated by Cody. He wasn’t sure what to make of the news, but if it proved to be true, Terry would have no trouble believing Cody was behind it.

Cody froze, his expression one of pure disbelief when he turned to face the group.

“No!” he gasped. “No, he can’t be.”

"Terry thinks you did it," remarked Raven, her eyes boring into the side of Terry's head.

He growled back at her, "I never once said anything of the sort."

Cody used an arm to support himself, sagging as his knees refused to support his weight. Raven ran to help him before he fainted outright.

"Oh, God," Cody moaned. He needed a few moments to recover, and when he looked up from his hunched position, he asked, "Was it an accident? Do we know what happened? What was he doing on the beach?"

Raven glared at Rodney. "Well?"

Pinned in place by three sets of eyes, Rodney blurted, “I don’t know. All Stacey said was that Chris was found dead at the beach this morning.”

“That’s it?” Cody challenged, straightening to his full height. “That’s all she had to say. How did she know about it if no one else here does?”

His eyes popped as he remembered something else, “She said the body was found by an old man. That’s how she knew.”

“Old man?” questioned Raven, her mind flitting back to her reason for entering the kitchen. “There’s an old man in the shop who knows we are supplying the royal family.”

"What!" Cody gripped her right bicep tightly enough to make her squirm against the pain.

"Cody, you're hurting me."

"How could an old man know about the royal contract? Huh? How? No one knows but the four of us."

Everyone noticed that he said four, already reducing the number from five without having to mention Chris's death.

Still fighting to get free, Raven hissed, "I don't know, Cody. I don't have any idea who he is."

Sneering into her face and showing his teeth as he turned his gaze upon the other conspirators, Cody said, "Well, we'd better all take a good look, hadn't we."

Rodney was foolish enough to ask, "Why?"

Cody dropped his grip on Raven's arm so he could grab the back of Rodney's neck. Using the hold to march Rodney across the kitchen, he peered through the gap to see the customers in the shop.

"Because we're going to kill him. That's why."

The Paradox

Albert felt a brief flutter of panic when he saw Sergeant Andrews heading his way. She was no longer in the company of the barely legal age constable with the red cheeks and had Constable Thorpe with her instead. There could be no question she was heading his way; she was already looking through the windows of the pasty shop as she made her way alongside it.

Two police officers who knew him by two different names. Albert cursed under his breath for his stupidity. Drawing a slow, calming breath, he looked down at the pasty display.

The sound of voices in the backroom continued to drift out. There was an argument occurring, that was for certain, though Albert could only guess what it might be about. It wasn't to do with his whispered revelation because it was already raging before he came into the shop.

Regardless, he had to leave now.

Attracting the attention of the teenager, whose name badge he could now see displayed 'Pamela', he asked, "I'll take one of the steak and stilton pasties, please?"

He did so just before Sergeant Andrews rounded the corner and stepped into the shop.

"Oh?" replied Pam. "You don't want to wait for Raven now?"

Her question necessitated a response, but he no longer wished to speak for fear Sergeant Andrews might recognise his voice or his accent.

Flicking his eyes to the kitchen, Albert could see faces peering through the gap. The argument had ceased, and the back scenes workers were all staring right at him.

He'd gotten their attention sure enough, and that was a good thing, but now was not the time to press home his advantage. To do so would surely expose him to the police.

Faking an Irish accent and doing a terrible job of it, Albert said, "Yes, the steak and stilton pasty, to be sure."

Mercifully, Pamela couldn't have cared less that the old man with the terrifying clown makeup was now doing something strange with his voice. She scooped a pasty using a pair of stainless-steel tongs, dropped it into a paper bag that immediately showed grease spots and rang up the sale.

Albert handed over a five pound note and made sure to pirouette away from the police so they never saw his face.

Sergeant Andrews replaced Albert at the counter, already speaking to the girl behind it by the time he reached the door. He paused, one foot on the step as he listened to confirm she was there to officially break the news about Chris Mason and to begin establishing not only his movements, but those of the persons closest to the victim.

One thing it meant for certain was that Albert wasn't going to get to speak to any of the pasty shop workers any time soon. He would have to return later and hoped he would be able to utilise Stacey to assist with setting that up.

Looking around once he was a good distance from Terry's shop and the police inside, Albert took a bite of pasty and wondered where Stacey and Rex had gone.

At that precise moment, Stacey was peering around the plastic curtain at the back of the pasty shop. Her heart beat out a rhythm so fast and so hard she thought it might explode and she was on the cusp of abandoning her plan to rescue the dog when she saw his head appear.

"Rex!" she hissed, combining a desire to not be heard with an urgent need to attract the dog's attention.

Rex heard his name and glanced to find the woman his human had left him with. She was making beckoning motions, imploring him to come to her. Should he go? Or continue his investigation. While Stacey grimaced and begged, Rex gave himself a moment to think.

There were four humans in the kitchen now and the one who recently arrived was the same man who left his smell on the murder victim's clothes. That didn't mean he was the killer, and Rex could detect no trace of blood in the air when the man went by. He needed time to consider what he knew and also to liaise with his own human who Rex had just seen leaving the shop via the front door.

Accepting the situation for what it was, Rex took a pace to his left, moving away from Stacey who hissed his name and increased the urgency of her motions. Without taking his eyes from the four humans – Rex could see the backs of their heads as they talked to someone unseen in the shop, he lifted his head, bit hold of the nearest pasty, and trotted merrily toward Stacey and the exit.

Stacey had several choice expletives to share with Rex, grabbing his lead and keeping a tight grip this time. Her plan was to drag him through the yard and into the street, but Rex needed no encouragement.

The pasty in his mouth was too hot for Rex to hold which necessitated careful use of just his teeth. Holding his tongue and jowls away from the hot pastry wasn't easy and gave his face a mad expression. In turn this helped to create a path through the crowd, for those who saw him coming chose to step to one side.

Rex spotted Albert first, his tail wagging happily and his pace quickened to close the final yards.

Albert was halfway through his own pasty and seeing that Rex had one of his own, couldn't resist the laugh that burst from his lips.

"Got away from you, did he?" Albert asked, swallowing a mouthful of too-hot meaty filling.

Stacey frowned at the old man in the clown suit.

"You could have mentioned that he might try to do something like that."

"There's something going on at the pasty shop," Albert remarked to steer the conversation on a new course.

Beneath the humans, Rex dropped his pasty to the ground where it split open and followed it down, nudging it about with his nose to spread the pieces. The cobbles were cold and would help to cool the filling to eating temperature. Not that he was prepared to wait. A scalded tongue was a worthy battle scar in the fight against hunger.

Not that Rex had any real idea what hungry was. Like most dogs, he ate defensively. If there was food and he wasn't full to the point of discomfort, he would eat it because one never knew how long it might be until the next meal.

While the humans talked, he made short work of the meat, potato, and pastry mix.

Stacey and Albert were arguing about what to do next. Albert couldn't go to the police: Stacey understood that, but couldn't fathom why Albert didn't want her to approach them in his stead when she promised to keep his name out of it.

"But you will most likely ruin the best chance I have to clear my name. If I am right, and all indications are that Terry's Pasty Shop is the Gastrothief's next target, then I ..."

"Hold on. The what? Did you just say 'Gastrothief?"

Albert sighed both physically and mentally. When he coined the name, it was never supposed to be one he shared with anyone else. At the time he wanted a mental reference for what he was seeing, and Gastrothief – because the crimes were all linked to food or the food industry – fitted nicely.

It was only afterward when he foolishly employed the name when talking to his son, Gary, that the absurdity of it dawned.

"Yes," Albert admitted. "I had to call the person behind the crimes something. It's not a great name, but it's the one I picked. The point is this: someone out there has been orchestrating a series of crimes involving food. Wine, cheese ... speciality food stuffs have all been going missing along with the equipment and raw ingredients required to make more of the same, and the people who know how to do it. That person is my stupidly named Gastrothief. I don't want to use the term 'master criminal'," Albert made air quotes, "but whoever it is has people working for them. They do the dirty work and I have already bumped into more than one pair of these 'agents'." More air quotes. "They stake out a place, learn the routine, and then grab what they need. They pose as regular folks, find a person working at the firm and ask them questions. I think that person was Chris Mason."

Stacey was doing her best to follow Albert's logic.

"You think the pasty shop is being targeted by a master criminal who is going to … what? Kidnap the people working there and steal the ovens?"

Albert flapped his arms out to his sides in an exaggerated shrug.

"Something like that. I saw this exact same pattern in Kent a week ago." Or was it two, he questioned in his head. The days all seemed to blur into one. "If Chris got suspicious, they would have killed him. Leaving the body to be found is a bit clumsy, but I guess they wanted it to look like an accident."

"How do you know it wasn't?"

"Because Chris Mason can't swim, and he was at the beach in a pair of tiny swimming trunks when it's only a few degrees above freezing at that time of day. He was murdered." Albert concluded.

It was information overload so far as Stacey was concerned; her mind awash with crazy new concepts to dissect and reject.

"Hold on," she found her way back to the start of the conversation. "You started off by saying there is something going on at the shop. In fact, I told you there was something going on there. My brother is being secretive about something, and it can't be anything to do with this Gastrothief, can it?" She pointed out, then questioning her own logic, added, "Can it?"

Four feet south, Rex's head had just come off the ground. The pasty was gone, but miniscule traces of flavour clung to the cobbles which were getting a damned good lick courtesy of his rough tongue. He stopped instantly when a familiar scent hit his nose.

Albert heard Rex's low growl, the same one he displayed outside their bed and breakfast this morning, but he didn't look down. He couldn't.

Dangerous Waters

Rooted to the spot, Albert willed his feet to move, but they were stuck firm. He willed his mouth to operate, but his brain had downed tools and was refusing to play.

Worried the old man might be having a stroke, Stacey asked, "Are you all right?" Albert had gone very still, and his expression hadn't changed at all in the last half dozen seconds.

Rex got to his feet. His lips were pulled back to reveal his teeth and his hackles had raised to create a ridge of proud fur along his spine. He couldn't see the woman he knew was somewhere close by, but Albert could.

Spotting Tanya ought to have come as a relief – it meant he was right. Right about the Gastrothief sending people to Looe. Right about the timing. Right about everything. Not only were they here right now, but he had found them.

His right hand twitched, wanting to take out his phone and call the police.

Tanya hadn't spotted him, but watching her from behind his disguise, even while his heart regained its normal rhythm, he could see that she was looking for someone. Tanya's behaviour stood out from the people around her. Where they were browsing in windows and almost entirely in pairs or small groups, she was by herself and her eyes were roving the people around her, not the goods on sale.

Rex took a pace forward. Tanya's scent was being carried on the breeze coming off the quay by the fish market. And it was getting stronger.

Rex's movement broke Albert's reverie just when Stacey lifted a hand to click her fingers in his face.

"I've just spotted one of the Gastrothief's agents," he murmured, refusing to take his eyes from Tanya.

"Ooh, where?"

With a jolt, Albert questioned where her partner was. Already convinced Baldwin was too badly injured in their last encounter to be here now, that didn't mean Tanya wasn't with someone new.

Albert had no idea how it worked, but in the moment that her roving gaze swung in his direction, Albert turned his head away. He didn't want to risk locking eyes with her, which might happen if she saw him looking directly at her, but also he hoped he might spot a second person acting just like Tanya – her partner.

"Albert," Stacey hissed at him. "Who are you talking about?"

Hissing back, Albert begged, "Don't use my name. She knows it."

Rex was straining at his lead, his front paws coming off the ground as he tried to intercept the woman he saw as a threat.

“That’s her!” he whined, getting ready to bark. “That’s the woman who shot me!” He was still angry about being tagged with a taser.

Certain Rex would give him away as surely as if he had not changed his appearance, Albert put a hand over the dog’s muzzle and coaxed him back around the side of a stall selling rubbish jewellery made from forks. Tanya came by the spot they’d occupied a moment later, oblivious that she had passed less than three feet from her target.

Exhaling a breath he’d been holding for most of a minute, Albert sagged before pushing himself upright again.

"That's Tanya. I don't know her last name, but she's a hired killer and about as dangerous as they come."

Stacey's eyebrows formed a deep 'V'. "Really? She doesn't look like much. She can't weigh more than a hundred pounds." Stacey was actually thinking she could kick Tanya's butt, but felt it sounded juvenile to say so.

Albert started walking, following Tanya now that she had a few yards lead on him.

From the side of his mouth, he said, "I need to know where she is going."

Stacey caught Albert's arm, stopping him. "You said you were going to help me with my brother. What about the pasty shop and whatever it is he's mixed up in?"

Meeting her angry expression with kindly eyes, Albert gently took her hand from his arm.

"If I go in there now, I'll get arrested and I'll be no use to you at all. I will happily talk to your brother later and do my best to figure out if there is anything to figure out." Nodding his head down the street in Tanya's general direction, he said, "The clues point to the Gastrothief's involvement. I need to follow Tanya. If I can find out who she is working with and where they are staying, I can catch them in the act, blow the whole case open, and prevent them from enacting whatever plan it is they have for your brother's pasty shop. You can help me."

Stacey couldn't figure out whether the old man was making the whole thing up or if perhaps he was the only person on the planet who truly knew what was happening.

Reluctantly though, she nodded her head and went with him.

Rex led the way, his nose guaranteeing they wouldn't lose their quarry and could minimise the likelihood of being spotted, whilst keeping their distance.

However, while the daft clown suit, wig, and makeup had done a marvellous job of concealing his identity from Tanya, he was one hundred percent wrong about not being spotted. Oh, Tanya wouldn't see him, but after slipping out the back of the pasty shop while the police talked to the others, Cody had no trouble at all in finding the person Raven described.

That the old man was with Stacey caused a ripple of anger to cross Cody's face. The old man knew about the royal engagement order, and it didn't take the brains of an archbishop to figure out he had obtained that snippet of vitally important information from Rodney's sister.

Cracking his knuckles, Cody kept his distance. He was going to find out who the old man was, where he was staying, and then pay him a little visit in the dead of the night.

Elevenses

Many miles away from Cornwall, but also not that far when viewed on a global scale, Earl Hubert Bacon dabbed at his face with a silk napkin. A few crumbs tumbled from one of his chins, landing on his shirt where his bulbous belly stretched the fabric outward.

Reaching to his right with a pudgy hand, he picked up his handheld vacuum cleaner and proceeded to remove the waste of his elevenses.

The Cornish pasty, a choice inspired by recently discovering his distant relative, Prince Marcus, was to marry a commoner who had chosen the treats to be served at a party for their engagement, had bridged the gap between second breakfast and luncheon.

He'd always planned to 'save' a Cornish pasty maker, and only changed his initial selection, an award-winning family located in Falmouth, upon hearing the news about Marcus and his riffraff oik of a girl. She was a lawyer or something, apparently.

The invitation to their engagement party arrived less than three days ago – the whole thing was very hush hush as if they believed they could keep it from the press. Well, the press wouldn't hear it from Hubert Bacon, that was for sure.

Kelly and Liam were in Cornwall to get him the people working at Terry's Pasty Shop in the centre of Looe. A smile creased the Earl's face when he thought about how his scheme would throw a spanner in Norma Morley's plans.

"Ideas above her station," he commented to himself.

One of the house chefs cleared away the Earl's plate and brushed a few remaining crumbs from the table. Not given to linger, the chef retreated in a hurry when the Earl, who was given to expel his excess gas as and when he felt the need to do so, unashamedly let one rip.

The pasty makers would join his happy throng of workers and would survive the holocaust by staying safe in the Earl's underground bunker. In return for their safety and long life, he would get Cornish pasties whenever he wanted them. It wasn't even nearly a fair trade, but he didn't mind.

His agents would burn the shop to the ground ensuring no one else would ever enjoy the delicacies he chose for his larder. For him it added an immeasurable quality to his food – he was the only one in the world able to eat the foods he had. He wished he'd thought to start destroying premises sooner.

With nothing but happy thoughts in his head, Earl Bacon began to consider his lunch options.

Who is Following Who?

As Albert expected, following Tanya was easy. She checked her rear many times, but if she thought there was anything suspicious about the clown following her, she did an impressive job of hiding it. Albert knew he would stick out but there were so many people in the street all heading one way or the other, that he believed it wouldn't matter. In a way he was conspicuously invisible.

Employing an old trick, Albert had Stacey buy two candyfloss on sticks. The sticky, pink treat wasn't for eating though; its purpose was to hide their faces. They could talk and from a distance, it would just look like they were eating.

Tanya poked her head into shops, looking inside but rarely going much beyond the threshold.

“What’s she looking for?” Stacey chose to ask not long after they began tailing the diminutive career criminal.

Albert allowed a wry smile to touch his eyes.

“Me.”

It was a simple statement and one that encapsulated everything his life had become on his trip around the UK. Not for the first time, Albert questioned what he might be doing today if he had just chosen to keep his nose out of the mysteries he stumbled across.

"You?"

"Me. My need for disguise wasn't just to keep the police from my door. That reminds me, I need to move out of my lodgings. The police will look for me there – they'll want to record a statement about how I found Chris Mason's body. I gave them a false name."

Stacey almost asked why he would do that.

Tanya led them all the way along Fore Street until it became Buller Street. There she turned left onto Higher Market Street which was also beset with stalls in the middle of the road and businesses to either side.

Fervently, Albert prayed she would lead them to her lodgings so he might know where to watch later, or that she would meet with her handler – the person who gave her orders. There had to be someone, and clawing his way up a tier as he attempted to bring down the Gastrothief's empire held delightful promise.

One of Albert's greatest concerns was that he would catch Tanya in the act of kidnapping and be able to bring the authorities down on her head only to then discover she knew too little to be of any use. What if the Gastrothief managed her through a handler just as Albert suspected, but did so in order that she couldn't reveal any worthwhile information if she was ever to be caught?

It was enough to keep him awake at night.

Nevertheless, now that he was on her tail, he felt buoyed by hope. This was better than he could have dreamed. All he had to do was be patient – a task far harder than it sounded – and she would show him all he needed to know. Armed with knowledge, he would call the police and proudly present the real bad guys as they perpetrated their crimes.

Waiting until Tanya was launching her attack ran the risk of placing people in danger, but he hoped that through Stacey, he would be able to warn and prepare them. It was a cagey game, he acknowledged that, but could see no alternative.

How soon would it be? Well, if pushed for an answer, Albert's guess would be tonight. As soon as tonight. Tanya wasn't here for the sea air or for the festival as evidenced by watching her walk by every stall in the town without pausing once to sample anything.

Rex kept his nose in the air and stayed close to his human. The woman they were tracking had almost hurt the old man more than once and Rex's natural protective streak was running deeper than usual.

The murder was something he planned to return to if there was time, but even though his canine brain could not comprehend the complexity of the crimes Tanya was involved in, he knew she was bad news and a person to be stopped.

The moment his human told him to go, Rex would chase down the woman and he wouldn't let her go until the police came; just like he'd been trained.

Without warning, Albert reached out with one hand to stop Stacey as he himself halted.

"Hold on," he insisted, speaking at a barely audible volume even though he wouldn't have been heard by Tanya unless he was to shout.

"What is it?" Stacey asked, masking her face with the candy floss.

Albert nodded his head in Tanya's direction, unwilling to take his eyes off her.

Tanya had reacted to someone she could see, her pace quickening. At least, that's what Albert believed he was witnessing, his patience rewarded a moment later when she tapped a man on his shoulder and began speaking.

The man turned to face Tanya, responding to whatever she had said.

A grin spread across Albert's face. "Bingo."

Just ahead of him a small girl squealed and clung to her mother, forcing Albert to drop the smile.

Stacey still didn't know why they had stopped or what might have caused Albert's jubilant expression.

"She just met with two people who know her." Albert turned side on, so he wasn't staring at them. "They are agents of the

Gastrothief," he announced confidently."

"Or they could be a couple she met in a bar last night."

Albert shook his head. They were the right age, the right demographic, and the new couple was not acting like a … couple. Even ones who had been married for years would be standing closer to one another.

Taking out his phone, he asked, "Can you help me? I need to get pictures of them. How do I do the zoom in thing?"

He offered his phone to Stacey with an apologetic smile.

"You need to stop doing that," Stacey frowned as she took the phone. "Your make up isn't designed for smiling. I'm going to have nightmares for weeks. There." She handed the phone back having snapped half a dozen shots of the people Albert wanted.

Albert was about to say they might need to split up if Tanya and her new friends went in separate directions when his eyes caught sight of someone else.

"Well, I'll be …" he muttered angrily.

The skinny kid who stole his wallet was lounging against a wall just beyond Tanya and the couple she was talking to. Wearing the exact same clothes as last night, Albert could have picked him out of a line up with ease.

Pushing off with a foot that had been resting against the brickwork, the pickpocket picked an angular path through the crowd, bumped a lady walking arm in arm with her husband/boyfriend and swiped a purse from her open handbag while apologising for his clumsiness.

Albert spat bullets.

Constantly questioning her decision to help the old man, Stacey groaned, "What now?"

He knew he couldn't really afford to draw attention to himself, but Albert was too incensed to stop.

With a gentle tug on Rex's lead to get him moving, Albert stalked toward a stall selling sausages. The goods on display were raw, but the butcher selling them was savvy enough to have some cooking on a hotplate. The smell drew in the customers who could then taste the wares before purchase.

“Pay attention, Rex,” Albert advised, leading his dog toward the stall. He cut his eyes to the left, making sure Tanya was still there. Relieved to see she hadn’t moved, Albert nudged his way toward the hotplate, gave the stallholder a nod, and took a cocktail stick on which a ready cooked piece of sausage was impaled.

Rex’s eyes locked on to it like a fighter plane’s radar system acquiring a target. His paws did a little dance, and his tongue licked all the way around his mouth as he began to salivate.

Was it for him?

Albert blew on the piece of meat, turning away from the stall to shield his actions. Timing it, he watched the pickpocket strolling unabashed away from his latest victim. The woman had noticed her missing purse now and had stopped in the street to root through her handbag.

As her motions became frantic, Albert removed the cocktail stick and threw the piece of succulent meat.

Rex could not have resisted chasing it if he tried.

The morsel prescribed an arc as it fell lazily toward the earth. Rex lunged while at the same time Albert gripped the dog lead with both hands and leaned back.

The lead went taut at the exact moment the pickpocket was passing through the patch of air that had been empty half a second previously.

Rex felt something tug on his neck, but the only thing going through his mind was the piece of sausage. With a gulp it was gone, barely tasted, but cherished, nonetheless.

Twisting to see if there was anymore, Rex found a skinny youth lying on the ground under his tail.

“I’ll take that, thank you,” Albert snatched the ladies’ purse from inside the pickpocket’s thin jacket. He really wanted to make sure the kid was arrest-ed, but doing so would allow Tanya and her colleagues to elude him and once again place him in direct contact with the police.

Grabbing the youth's shoulder in a vice grip as he attempted to flee, Albert snarled, "Next time you go to jail." Then, with a shove, he sent the pickpocket running.

"Do I chase?" asked Rex, on his feet and ready to go. "And bite?" he added hopefully. That it was the same human he'd chased and lost last night had not eluded him and he felt a little let down that his nose failed to detect the kid's scent earlier. "Distracted by sausage," he harrumphed to himself.

Albert watched, annoyed that he felt forced to let the delinquent criminal go.

A few yards back along Higher Market Street, Cody observed the event and questioned just what he was seeing. The clown outfit was bewildering. No matter who the man inside it was, the choice of outfit was bizarre. He was poking into affairs he should have no knowledge of and that alone ought to make him want to be inconspicuous.

Why had he chosen to make himself so visible?

Was he police? Counter terrorism? How much had Rodney told his sister? The answer to the last question was one Cody planned to obtain soon. He would invite Rodney to come for a little walk. Terry wouldn't like it – the business was about as busy as it ever got, but the concept of their plans outweighed the sale of a few pasties.

Every time Cody saw the punters handing over notes with the Queen's head smiling out at him, he wanted to scream in their faces. The more money they made, the madder he became.

Terry could make money later. Cody would help. Once they'd toppled the class system wasting so much of the taxpayers' money, Cody would make sure his oldest friends ... those who supported and shared his cause, would be rewarded.

He would take Rodney to his boat. Yeah, that's what he would do. Rodney was too dumb to suspect anything was amiss and would be at sea with the business end of a bat aimed at his head before he realised just how much trouble he was in.

Cody's feet twitched, eager to get back to the shop and to Rodney, a person already labelled as 'traitor' in Cody's mind, but the man in the clown suit continued to hold his interest.

Just as Cody was tailing him, the clown looked to be tailing someone else. It had taken a while to figure it out, but the clown had just set off again, following a man and a woman as they meandered toward the coast. A second woman had been talking to them a moment ago, but was heading in a different direction now.

That was how Cody managed to figure out what the clown was doing – he'd ducked out of the second woman's path, darting out of sight as she came his way.

Stacey didn't duck though; she stayed where she was.

Cody deliberated for a moment, but no longer. The old man had said something to Stacey and now the two of them were following the couple.

He tagged along to see where they might be going.

Big Sister Power

Stacey handed the recovered purse back to its owner, saying, "Did you drop this?" Albert convinced her it was the best thing to do. She believed she recognised the pickpocket, but couldn't be certain. Either way, Albert promised to deal with him if he could clear his name and believed he was on the cusp of doing just that.

Resolved to help Albert, yet ever mindful that she was more interested in finding out if her brother was getting himself into trouble, Stacey called Rodney's phone.

"Rodney, are you busy?"

"Of course I'm busy! It's one of the busiest times of the year! Terry's got us working flat out and Chris … well, you already know about Chris. We're short-handed."

"But you have to get a lunchbreak, don't you?"

Begrudgingly, Rodney admitted, "Yes. It's going to be a short one though and the police have had us all tied up for the last twenty minutes, asking questions about Chris. They want proper statements from all of us about our movements last night and this morning. I …" Rodney had been about to question what he was supposed to tell the police when he stopped himself.

He shared everything with his sister, he always had done. She was older than him by five years and had always looked out for him. Now he had a secret he was supposed to keep from her.

Cody made it very clear what the consequences might be for telling anyone what he had planned. That was before the plan became reality, of course. That was when it was all talk. It was nothing more than conversation in a corner of the pub until just a couple of days ago. At least that's what Rodney believed.

Cody hated the royal family; not that he ever fully explained why, and Terry agreed. That was enough to make Rodney play along though he had no real opinion of his own. But the talk of one day rising up to bring down the classist system oppressing common man and keeping working folk under the boot had suddenly changed.

The vitriol didn't change but the ability to act was unexpectedly thrust into their faces. How Cody's eyes had gleamed at the opportunity to strike right at the heart of all that he hated.

"You were saying something?" Stacey prompted.

"No, I … ah, I … what do you need, Stacey?" Rodney tried not to snap impatiently. On edge though and with multiple demands on his time, he did just that.

"Brother, you need to watch your tone," Stacey had played extra mum to Rodney most of her life even though their mum was alive and well and living in the house they grew up in along with their father. "I need ten minutes of your time. It's VERY important. When do you get a break?"

Letting his shoulders droop and not bothering to fight simply because he knew he would lose, Rodney said, "Twelve o'clock, Stacey. I can take a break at twelve."

"I'll be waiting at my shop. Don't be late," she warned in a big sister tone. "Or I'll come and drag you out of that pasty shop by your ear."

Rodney had a response to give but Stacey had already ended the call. The worst thing was that he knew she would do it. She'd done it before, and she detested everyone he worked with. Especially Terry. Rodney wasn't sure why and no one would tell him, but Terry gave Stacey a wide berth, so he was certain that she would deliver on her threat if he failed to arrive on time.

Annoyed, he slammed the next tray of pasties into the oven with double the required force, spilling three from the front end when the laws of physics demonstrated how inertia works.

A Focal Point

Albert watched the couple Tanya met as they talked to multiple stallholders and spotted a pattern very quickly: they bought nothing, they tasted nothing, and they only talked to cider producers.

To anyone else it might have seemed innocuous. Albert knew better. He still believed his hunch about the pasty shop was bang on, but now he'd identified a secondary target. Or maybe it was tertiary, he couldn't know for sure.

One thing he did know was that the man and woman were acting like no one else in the town. All around them, the hungry visitors were vying to sample the foods on offer or the beverages, which were being quaffed from plastic pint 'glasses' in every direction. Everyone carried bags filled with the goodies they'd purchased.

All except the Gastrothief's agents. No power on earth would convince Albert he was wrong.

"Is there a cider making competition?" Albert asked, quizzing Stacey now that her phone call had finished.

Stacey cast her eyes up and to the right, engaging her memory.

"Yes, I believe so."

Albert nodded to himself. That was it then. They were going to kidnap a cider maker and probably their stock, possibly driving away in the van the brewer came in.

It explained why they hadn't hit the pasty shop yet. Or, rather, it provided one possible explanation - they needed to get all their ducks in a row before striking.

"How long are we going to follow them for?" Stacey asked, doing nothing to hide her mounting frustration. It was coming up on eleven thirty and she wanted Albert to speak with Rodney far more than she cared to follow a potential criminal around her hometown.

Half of the people she knew had already spotted her with the clown and asked what she was up to. It was going to take a lot of explaining if he did anything while still wearing it.

Albert spoke from the side of his mouth. “I need to know where they are staying.” He was beginning to worry his local aide would grow too impatient and force him to go elsewhere before he knew where to reacquire the agents. If he knew where they were staying, he would have options and know where to look for them. He imagined being able to sneak a look at the hotel’s registry, or perhaps slip someone a few notes to give him their names.

Upon thinking that, another idea popped into his head.

“How sure are you that you know who that young pickpocket was?”

Stacey's face crinkled. "What? What does that have to do with anything? Look, Albert, you promised to help me find out whether my brother is in trouble, and so far all we have done is follow people around Looe. In half an hour he is going to be at my shop, and you had better be there too. Or else I might feel a need to make an anonymous phone call."

Albert stopped what he was doing and turned to face Stacey.

"I'm sorry. You are right. I believe that I am helping. In all likelihood the people I am tailing are responsible for the murder of Chris Mason ..."

"You don't know that it was murder," Stacey argued angrily.

Albert accepted her point.

"No, but I believe it was. I can offer you no hard evidence and that is precisely why I find myself in my current predicament. If they killed Chris Mason, then they plan to raid the pasty shop with a view to kidnapping at least one person capable of producing the pasties you claim are favoured by Prince Marcus's fiancé. It might be your brother they take. I only ask that you bear with me a short while longer." As he ended his sentence, Albert twisted to check he still had the couple in sight.

He didn't.

"Where'd they go!" he blurted, gawping down the street and ducking left and right to spot them.

In the ten seconds he'd been focused on Stacey, they had vanished.

Panic rising, he ran between two stalls to look on the other side of the street. They were not there either.

Forcing himself to calm, he turned to Rex.

Rex had been obediently trailing along at his human's side. Content to be outside and exploring, he had expressed his confusion at letting Tanya walk away, and questioned what Albert might be up to. It was only due to his belief that the old man was capable and most likely had a plan Rex didn't understand that he let Albert get on with it.

Following them was the man who'd left his scent on the dead man's clothing.

Rex had tried to point this out to his human more than once to no avail and might have made a bigger issue of it if he felt convinced it was important.

The man's scent was on the murder victim's clothing, that made him interesting, but nothing more. His human did not appear to be trying to solve the murder though and it caused Rex to question what he ought to do.

Now his human was coming down to Rex's level.

"Rex, lad, I need you to find someone. Can you do that?"

Rex wagged his tail. "Finding people is my specialty. Have you got something of theirs? I need it to be able to track their scent."

Albert said, "The couple we've been following, boy. Can you find them?"

Rex wagged his tail again, but stopped abruptly.

"You don't have anything with their scent on, do you? I'm not a miracle worker, man. I mean, meet me halfway at least.

Failing to understand the noises coming from Rex, Albert used both hands on his knees to push himself back to upright and thrust out an arm, urging Rex to, "Get with the sniffing."

Rex stared up at Albert and gave brief consideration to lifting a back leg on his garish clown trousers.

When Rex failed to move, Albert looked down and would have asked why his dog wasn't searching for the bad guys had Stacey not reappeared.

"They went this way," she announced.

Knowing the town as she did, Stacey's local knowledge told her there was only one place the couple might have gone when they abruptly vanished.

As Higher Market Street turned to track the coastline, a narrow alley cut through to a pair of hotels nestled on the cliffs. Enjoying dominant views overlooking the sea, the couple could have gone into either one. Stacey got it right the first time, spying the man heading into an elevator just as she stepped into reception.

A young man at the reception desk had looked up with a smile of greeting only for it to turn to a one eyebrow question when Stacey performed a prompt about-face.

Hoping she could satisfy Albert's need to know where the couple were staying, even though she wasn't entirely convinced the whole Gastrothief thing didn't exist only in his head, she led him to the end of the alley and pointed.

"That one. Cliff View Hotel and Spa. Not that it's got a spa. Not unless you call a sauna the size of a cupboard and a pool that will fit four people a spa. Anyway," Stacey realised she was embellishing her point senselessly. "They went in there and got into an elevator. Good enough? Can we go now?" Checking her watch, she said, "We've got twenty minutes to get back to my shop."

Albert sucked on his teeth. What he really wanted to do was enter the hotel and carefully ask some pointed questions. He couldn't do that in a clown suit though, not if he wanted to get answers. Like it or not, he needed to do as Stacey asked. It was that or risk losing her as a local guide with the added worry that she might go ahead and call the police.

"Yes," he replied, heading back along the alley to Higher Market Street. "I feel it is also time for me to change my outfit. Plus," he talked as his mind worked, "I need to vacate my accommodation."

"Yes, you said that earlier," Stacey remembered. "Where are you staying?"

Loose Lips

Stacey knew all the shortcuts, taking Albert on what he thought at first was a circuitous route until it landed him outside his bed and breakfast less than a minute later.

"Golly," he murmured, seeing where he was. It was then that his memory chose to supply a fun snippet of detail. With a groan, he revealed, "I don't have my key. It's in my trousers."

Stacey didn't even break stride.

"It's a good thing that I know where Joseph keeps his spare then, isn't it."

Stacey marched directly up to the bed and breakfast, bypassing the front door and leaning over a narrow flower bed to extract a loose brick from the base of the wall.

Five seconds later, the key was back where it belonged, and Albert was inside. He left Rex with Stacey once more, his dog frowning in a doggy-like manner, but obeying, nevertheless.

It wasn't so much that he didn't like or didn't trust his human's new companion, goodness knows there had been a selection of those in the last few weeks. It was more that he didn't know her, and his loyalty was to Albert. Rex cared about Albert, a human with a startling proclivity for landing himself in dangerous situations. For the most part Rex couldn't give a stuff about anyone else.

There were no sounds from within the house, which came as a relief to Albert. He pinched the spare key for his room from a hook in the kitchen and packed his bags quickly, hoping to avoid an encounter with the landlord. Had the police come by looking for him? He saw Sergeant Andrews heading in this direction earlier. So did she already discover he'd provided a false name this morning at the beach?

With no way of knowing, Albert crammed the last of his belongings into his backpack and ran for the door.

Then he ran back to collect the items he'd omitted to take from the bathroom and on his second attempt was successful in exiting the property.

Breathing a sigh of relief now that he was back in the street, he took Rex's lead once more and declining Stacey's offer to carry something, followed her back to the fancy dress shop.

"Are you not concerned about missed sales?" he asked, partly to make conversation and show interest, but also because it had just occurred to him that she had been out of her shop for the last hour and a half and had no assistant to take over that he had seen.

Stacey shrugged in a forlorn manner.

"Your sale this morning is the first in two weeks. That's from direct sales out of the shop. The shop is a total dead end.

I started advertising it on the internet though, there are several online shops that allow a person to set up a virtual storefront. Fancy dress costumes sell quite easily there but I came this close," she held up her right hand with the thumb and forefinger almost touching each other, "to defaulting on my loan. I paid up front for six months' rent because I got a good deal and I still have ten weeks to go, so I figure I might as well keep the shop open just in case anyone wanders in."

"You'll continue the business online when you shut the actual shop?" Albert asked, showing that he was paying attention while questioning if 'actual' shop was the opposite of 'virtual'.

Stacey lifted an arm to steer Albert down a street he was not about to take. "That's the plan."

Rex's nose was twitching. The man was still following them, the one whose scent was on the dead man's clothes. Rex still wasn't sure whether he ought to be investigating or not – his human didn't appear to be. In fact, the old man was far more interested in the woman Rex knew from previous encounters – Tanya, the name popped into Rex's head.

He knew the name because it had been said several times in direct reference to her. However, to drizzle further doubt into Rex's mind, his human had then abandoned following Tanya, to go after a new man and woman instead.

Content enough to play along, Rex decided that if he got the chance, he was going to see if he couldn't figure out who was behind the murder just to satisfy his own curiosity.

At the shop, Stacey unlocked the door and pushed it open, stepping to one side to allow Albert and Rex to enter while she checked her watch.

It was one minute after twelve, but as she swivelled around to glare at the windows of the pasty shop down the road, her brother appeared in the street.

His brow was streaked with sweat from the hot kitchen and there were visible damp patches under his arms. Hurrying down the street, a hair net still in place, Rodney tugged a thin jacket on over his work clothes. Embroidered across the left chest were the words 'Terry's Pasty Shop'.

Stacey held the door open, waiting for him to arrive.

"This had better be important, Sis. Terry is doing his nut."

"Can't the others cope for just a few minutes?"

"No." Rodney stated unambiguously. "Chris is dead, and Cody vanished more than an hour ago. Terry says he won't answer his phone."

Stacey's forehead wrinkled at the news and had been about to say something when she chose to hold back. It all came back to the people he worked with. Well, it was time to wheedle the truth out of him. She only hoped a seasoned police detective could achieve what she hadn't.

The door closed behind her, neither of them noticing the figure watching them.

Cody's hands were balled into fists. Rodney was working with them. There could be no doubt now. It was just a case of having loose lips, the man in the clown suit – Cody applauded the disguise now for he knew he wouldn't recognise the person beneath the makeup if he took it off – had to be working with special branch or whichever division of the police it was that was assigned to protect the royal family.

Rodney had chickened out of the plan. It would be Chris's fault; Cody knew how easily Rodney could be led. Rodney was foot soldier material – cannon fodder, where Cody thought of himself as the general. Like Oliver Cromwell, he planned to lead the nation to unite against their oppressors. That started with striking at the snake's head and he would not be denied because those around him were too weak to see the task through.

Filled with rage, Cody forced his eyes away from Stacey's shop door. He needed to get ready.

Lies

Albert emerged from the backroom dressed once more in his own clothes. In the small toilet located beyond the customer area of the shop, he'd found a sink and some soap. It dealt with the makeup more or less, not that Albert could see the bits he'd missed in the dim light coming from a low watt overhead bulb. Nevertheless, he looked like Albert again.

"Who's this?" Rodney wanted to know, spinning around when the door behind him unexpectedly opened.

Stacey did the introductions. "Rodders this is Albert. He's a friend of mine. Albert, please meet my brother. Rodney, Albert has a few questions for you."

"Are they the same questions you just asked?" Rodney snapped at his sister.

Waiting for Albert to finish getting dressed, Stacey had once again demanded to know what his idiot friends at the pasty shop were up to. She'd been nice about it then though. Now she let rip.

"Chris is dead!" Stacey pointed out, her voice rising with the exasperation she felt. "Someone killed him, Rodney."

Rodney eyebrows knitted into a frown.

"That's not what the police said. They told us he probably fell to his death, but they needed to investigate his recent movements to eliminate …"

"Any possibility of foul play," Albert finished the words he knew were coming. With Rodney now looking his way, Albert continued, "They say that because once you claim a person has been murdered it begins a chain of events that cannot be undone. Better to treat a death as suspicious and solve it before the press catch wind."

Rodney was defensive before the old man entered the room – his sister had seen to that with her insistence that he was lying to her. It went up a notch.

"So what are you saying? Do you think I killed Chris? He was my friend!"

Albert's years as a detective, the thousands of hours of interviews he'd conducted, allowed him to read Rodney. Stacey's younger brother was upset – naturally so following his friend's death this morning. The emotions battering his mind were causing him to lash out and right now he had a target whose feelings he didn't need to care about.

Offering the young man a sad smile, Albert said, "It's hard losing a friend. I've lost a few in the course of my life. His passing must have been quite a shock."

Thrown off balance by the old man's tone and choice of words – Rodney had expected to be shouted at and was ready to respond in kind – the wind in his sails deflated slightly.

His ire decreased further when Stacey put a gentle arm around his shoulders.

"Chris was a nice guy." Her words were softly spoken and laced with tender affection. "I liked him."

Rodney found himself adrift on a sea of sadness. The news had hit him like a bucket of ice water to the face, but in the face of the festival crowds and all the customers filing through the door, he had pushed his emotions aside to focus on doing as Terry asked – it was one of the busiest days of the year and Terry needed him. Now the truth of the situation hammered home and Rodney crumbled.

Pulled into Stacey's embrace, he cried, sobbing for a full five minutes before he gained control again.

When the crying subsided and Rodney gently levered himself away from his sister, Albert got down to business.

"Rodney, I have reason to believe a gang of criminals is targeting the shop in which you work. The people employed there, including you, may be in danger."

Albert waited a second for the words to sink in, watching Rodney's face as the questions formed. Before he was able to respond, Albert lifted his phone and started talking.

"Do you recognise either of these people?" he held the phone before Rodney's eyes, showing him Tanya, then the man she had met and then the woman who was with him. Albert watched Stacey's brother's eyes focus on each image in turn.

"Who are they?" Rodney asked, failing to answer Albert's question.

Keeping the phone raised, Albert said, "That's difficult to explain. Do you recognise any of them?" He scrolled the pictures using a finger and asked, "Has there been anyone in the shop asking questions about the business?"

Rodney looked up from the phone.

"What sort of questions?"

Albert lowered his phone. "Opening and closing times," he reeled off a short list of questions the staff at Porkers

Sausage Factory claimed Tanya and Baldwin asked. "Who knows the pasty recipe? Who gets into work first or leaves last? Anything like that."

Rodney didn't answer though it was not a conscious decision to do so. Confused by the line of questioning, he fired back one of his own.

"What is this all about?"

Unable to contain herself any longer, Stacey interrupted.

"What is the big secret you are all keeping, Rodney? I know you have been meeting after work. What is going on? Is it drugs? Are Terry and Cody smuggling drugs? Are you being used as a mule?"

"What? No! Why would you ever think we were doing anything with drugs?"

"Well, what is it then?"

"Nothing, Stacey. We are not doing anything."

"Liar!" Stacey spat the word and it echoed in the empty space of her shop. Silence fell.

Bringing the conversation down a notch, Albert said, "The people I just showed you are here right now in Looe. You undoubtedly saw that in the pictures. They are bad news. I don't have time to go into the whole story …" A memory surfaced. "Why don't you tell me what was happening at the shop last night?"

Stacey frowned. "Last night?"

Ignoring her, Albert pressed on with, "I saw you leaving last night. It was after nine o'clock." It was a white lie – he had seen no such thing, but his guess proved to be on the money.

"You were spying on us? Who are you?"

"Who is us?" Albert countered. Able to read Rodney well enough to know he wasn't going to answer, Albert said, "The police came, didn't they?" He already knew the answer to that one. "They got a report from someone that the premises might be getting burgled. I guess they saw lights in the basement long after the shop shut. Were you just having an after-work discussion in the lead up to the festival – working extra hours to be ready for today? Or had you been lured there by the people I showed you?"

Albert studied Rodney's face for any sign that he might have hit upon the truth.

"Yes," Rodney latched upon what felt like a lifeline. "Yes, that's what we were doing. Terry wanted to get as much done last night as could be. We all knew today would be busy." Rodney's words grew in confidence as the lie solidified in his mind.

However, Albert could hear the lie for what it was. He also recognised that in trying to ease the truth out, he'd provided a convenient line for Rodney to follow.

Changing tack, Albert came from a new angle, "Your sister told me about the royal wedding and how it is that your shop is going to supply pasties to the engagement party. Who else knows about it?"

Rodney blurted, "No one," his guilt and terror over telling Stacey forced the denial from his lips. "I shouldn't have told Stacey and I certainly haven't told anyone else."

Albert sucked some air in through his nose as he thought about what he knew and how he might use it. He was certain, despite what Rodney had to say, that the staff at Terry's Pasty Shop were about to get kidnapped. Some of them at least. Everything about the situation fitted, not least Rodney's own nervousness and need for secrecy. He knew something was going on; maybe they all had a sense of something out of place. Or was it that Rodney was the weak link, the loose lips? Had he told Tanya and company more than he should and now felt guilty?

"Rodney, if you have spoken to the people I showed you, you can tell us. It won't get you into trouble. It will be worse if you keep it a secret."

Stacey jumped in before her brother could answer.

"And please, Rodders, tell us what is going on at the shop. Cody and Terry are up to something. Did one of them kill Chris? What happened to him?"

Albert suspected Stacey was way off the mark about events at the shop. Why would someone there kill their friend and co-worker? Rather than reiterate his point about the Gastrothief's agents, Albert chose to let it go.

Rodney's phone rang, a sudden noise that made him jump.

"That will be Terry," he backed toward the door. "I have to go. I don't know anything about what the crazy old man is asking. I've never seen those people. We make pasties and we sell them. That's all."

There was no question he was lying, but when Stacey started forward to stop him leaving, Albert touched a hand to her arm. It delayed her by a second and that was all Rodney needed to get out of the door.

Turning to Albert, she vented her anger in his face.

"You let him go!"

Calmly Albert replied, "He's too scared to tell you the truth."

Stacey blinked. "Scared? Scared of what?"

Special Mission

"Hello, Rodney."

The sound of Cody's voice stopped Rodney's forward motion as effectively as a brick wall.

"Cody," he breathed the name.

"Yes," Cody placed a comradely arm around Rodney's shoulders. "We need to talk, you and I."

They were standing in the street halfway between Stacey's shop and their own place of work. People moved all around them, brushing past, but Rodney felt isolated from them somehow.

"Talk? I need to get back to work, Cody. Terry's been going mad that you vanished earlier."

Cody huffed a laugh like he thought Rodney's concerns were amusing.

"Terry understands the nature of the goal we are working toward. It is bigger than you or I. More important than a day's takings at a pasty shop. Come on, I have a special mission for you."

Cody used his arm to steer Rodney along the street. They passed the pasty shop with Rodney craning his neck in the hope Terry would see him and run out to ask Cody what he was playing at.

"I really ought to get back to the shop," he tried again.

"No!" Cody barked, then gave Rodney's shoulder a friendly squeeze. "No, Rodney. This is too important. If we don't act now, the chance will be missed."

"What chance? What is it that we need to do?"

Ignoring the question, Cody said, "We are soldiers you and I, Rodney. History will remember us, but only if we succeed. The cause is greater than the sum of its parts. Now quickly, Rodders. Time is of the essence."

Rodney had no idea where they were going, not until Cody steered him toward the quayside and the little fishing boat on which Cody lived. By then it was too late to argue. Too late to change a pattern of behaviour that had dominated his life. Rodney knew he was a coward and would always shy away from a fight. He also knew that going with Cody was the last thing he ought to be doing.

Meekly, he asked again where they were going and what it was that they needed to do, but was told to 'Get the lines'. They were going for a little trip out to sea.

A Plan. Of Sorts.

Stacey had her hands in her hair, gripping her skull as she worried herself almost sick.

"Do you really think this is all just to do with this … Gastrothief thing?"

Albert had chosen to sit in a handy chair by the window. His knees were aching a little from walking all morning and his back twinged from falling the previous evening. Rex was lying on the floorboards by his feet.

"Yes, Stacey, I do. It all fits. I cannot explain how they know about the royal engagement contract, but I must assume that they do. They will have looked for someone they could quiz about the business; that must have been Chris Mason. Your brother was, I'm afraid to say, lying about almost everything, but I saw his eyes when I showed him the pictures – he'd never seen Tanya or the other two before. Chris must have gotten suspicious or asked a question they didn't like. They killed him and staged his death. I hate to say that this is nothing new for them."

"They've killed people before?" Stacey's eyes widened.

Albert nodded, stroking Rex's head idly with one hand. "More than once." Truthfully, he could only guess what the body count might be and silently acknowledged that some of the dead were probably accidents like the wine connoisseur in Kent. "I believe they will strike tonight."

"Tonight! We must call the police!" Stacey took her hands from her head and yanked her phone from a back pocket.

"And tell them what?" Albert challenged, the timbre of his voice both calm and measured. "When they ask why you believe there is a plot to kidnap workers at a pasty shop, what will you tell them?" He cocked his head to one side, lifting his chin to encourage an answer. When none came, he said, "Exactly. Now you understand my predicament. Even if you introduce me into the equation, their focus will be on Albert Smith, not some wild conspiracy he has dreamed up. If they visit Terry's place, they are likely to tip off the Gastrothief's agents and the crime will never happen. That might sound like a good thing, but only for those few individuals. The Gastrothief will move on to his next target, whatever that might be. Worse yet, his agents may return here at any time."

"But we can't do nothing!"

Rising to his feet, Albert paced across the shop. "I am not proposing that we should. We have an advantage on our side."

"How so?" Stacey listened, her phone still poised in her right hand to make a call.

"The Gastrothief's agents have not the slightest idea we are watching them. Also, the town is crawling with police because of the festival and because they found a body on the beach this morning. We can do little in advance, other than position the pieces on the chess board."

Stacey choked out a laugh that contained no humour. "What does than even mean, Albert?"

"That we will be ready. We know where they are staying, and we know who they are after. I watched them scoping out the various cider makers today. There is only one reason for them to do that: they plan to grab the winner tonight after the results of the cider competition are announced. So now we know one more thing."

"Which is?"

"They will not strike until after they know who to take. They may come for the pasty makers first, but operating in such a tight environment, they risk exposure the moment they strike. They will have a plan to get away cleanly, but will not be able to predict all the variables. I will watch them, you will watch the pasty shop. When they make their move, we call the police."

"Really?" Stacey was genuinely surprised at Albert's simple plan.

He chuckled. "Yes, my days of taking criminals down myself are long behind me. They will be armed, and you will need to warn the police – embellish if you need to, say you think you saw guns."

“What if I do see guns?”

“Then you won’t be embellishing, will you?” Stopping his pacing right before Stacey, Albert looked directly into her eyes. “I cannot stress how dangerous this is. You must watch from a distance.”

“What are you going to do?”

Albert exhaled, giving himself just a moment to think. Sucking in a fresh lungful of air, he pulled himself up to his full height once more, telling himself he was near the end and in just a few hours he would be free to return home. He wasn’t tired. He wasn’t too old. He was perfectly capable of seeing it through to the end.

If only he could convince his body of the same.

"I am going to the Cliff View Hotel. I want to know the names of Tanya's colleagues. It may prove useful."

Stacey nodded her understanding and to her right, having heard Albert's announcement, Rex clambered to his feet.

Albert went to him, patting the dog on his head and lowering to one knee so he could meet Rex's gaze.

"Not this time, lad. If I can't be in disguise, I should at least not be seen with you. If anyone is looking for me, your big furry backside will make me much easier to pick out of a crowd. I'll only be a few minutes. Straight there and back, I promise."

Rex didn't like it, resting his head on Albert's knee and looking up at him with big, sorrowful eyes.

"You won't be safe without me, silly human."

Grabbing the arm of the chair, Albert ruffled Rex's fur and pushed himself upright.

To reassure Stacey, he paused at the door.

"I won't be long. This will be over soon. Remember, they have no idea they are being watched. This ends tonight."

"Don't you need to disguise yourself again?"

The question had been bugging Albert ever since he took the clown outfit off.

He believed the disguise had worked brilliantly … knew it had since Tanya walked right by him. However, if Tanya was to see the clown again, she would surely question why and the moment she paid attention she would see who was beneath the makeup.

There were other costumes he could wear, but to carefully extract information from staff at the Cliff View Hotel, he needed to look like a harmless old man. For this part of the adventure, he was going to have to be Albert and pray he avoided seeing anyone who might recognise him.

Looking around, Albert asked, “Do you have any hats?”

Worthless Information

Albert kept his head down and his feet moving when he left the shop. Rex had tried to force his way out when Albert opened the door and had to be held back by Stacey, one hand hooked through his collar until Albert could shut him inside.

A single glance over his shoulder revealed Rex in the shop's display window, knocking the mannequins over and barking his disapproval at Albert's plan to go alone.

Being out alone and looking like himself was just a risk he felt he had to take.

There were so many people in Looe he could lose himself amongst them, and he really wasn't going all that far.

Hurrying, but not at such a pace that he might draw attention to himself, he kept his eyes on the pavement. The tactic reduced the chance of making eye contact with Tanya if she was still out and about, but also increased the likelihood that he wouldn't see her first and be able to alter his course.

There was no good strategy to employ.

Despite his concerns, he made it to the hotel unimpeded just five minutes after leaving Stacey's shop. Breathing a mental sigh of relief, he stepped into the hotel's lobby and took off his hat.

Now he really looked like Albert Smith, so if Tanya was here and walked into the lobby, she would see him instantly.

Fixing a smile on his face, he aimed his feet at the hotel's reception desk.

The Cliff View Hotel was a year shy of being one hundred and fifty years old and its management were beginning to gear up for the big party they felt the place deserved. Between now and then, the décor in the central areas needed to be updated, and the front façade was to be jet washed from head to toe, returning some of the lustre years of seagull poop had removed.

The lobby was far removed from the modern high-ceilinged designs one would find in a new hotel and favoured dark oak and oil paintings in favour of chrome, glass, and cutting-edge touch-screen video displays.

The oak reception desk was an original feature carved from a single piece of wood. Behind it, head of day staff, Larry Johnson, reigned supreme, doing his utmost to shine for he had his eyes set on a management position.

Greeting the visitor with a professional smile– Larry knew upon sight that the old man approaching was not a guest at the hotel – he said, "Good afternoon, Sir. Welcome to the Cliff View Hotel. How many I assist you?"

Albert had his lines prepared in his head.

"Hello." He took out his phone. "My name is Roy Hope," he gave a false name again. "Wing Commander Roy Hope. I'm hoping you can help me to locate two people. I have some money for them."

It took him a moment to remember how to navigate to his photographs. However, once there he held up the picture of the man he'd seen talking to Tanya. Then when the man behind reception had seen it, he used a finger to scroll the screen to show the woman.

"I was at lunch and managed to forget my wallet. They were sitting at the next table and were kind enough to pay my bill. We argued about it, as you might imagine, but they were too fast for me, gave the waiter the money and with a generous smile they were gone."

Larry smiled indulgently. He could see where the story was going, but politely allowed the gentleman to continue.

"Well, I couldn't catch up with them, hence the pictures taken from a distance – my legs aren't what they used to be. But I heard them talking about this hotel; like I said, they were at the next table. Are they guests here?"

Larry considered the question for a moment. Under normal circumstances, he would never divulge any information about hotel guests. However, in this instance, it seemed harmless enough to answer a simple 'yes' or 'no' question.

"They are, Sir."

Smiling to show he was pleased with himself, Albert put his phone away and took out his wallet. Extracting two twenties, he asked, "Might you have an envelope I can put these in?"

Larry sidestepped to the far end of the desk and from a drawer withdrew a white rectangle.

Albert noted the high-quality paper from which it was made. To his mind a hotel that considered minor details like envelope quality was a place worthy of visiting.

He tucked the flap inside, but paused before handing it over.

With Larry's hand hovering in the air, Albert said, "I feel a need to write them a little note." He held up his right hand, miming holding a pen as a question.

Larry opened his jacket, selecting his ballpoint, not his Mont Blanc fountain pen which he refrained from handing to anyone. With a flourish, he clicked the end to extend the ball and held it out.

Albert nodded his thanks, fumbled for his reading glasses, and finally aligned himself to start writing.

"Their names," he prompted. "Is it Mr and Mrs?"

There were other customers behind Albert now, and Larry really wanted to move the older gentleman on. A vein flared in his neck, but convinced it was an insignificant and justified breach of guest privacy, he said, "Mr Baker and Miss Bancroft."

Pleased with himself, Albert made a show of noticing the other guests behind him.

"Oh, I'm holding up the line. I'll … um," he looked around, his eyes settling on a pair of chairs arranged around a low table. "I'll bring the pen back in a moment."

It was only when he surreptitiously slipped the twenties back into his wallet, that he realised how little worth the names were. When he first met Tanya and Baldwin, they had been using fake names. They did the same thing in Whitstable. Baker and Bancroft were no more likely to be genuine, but in that moment when he accepted how wasted his efforts were, he hit upon a plan that had a far higher probability of success. It would involve a criminal act and for once in his life, Albert was absolutely fine with that.

Returning the envelope and the pen, Albert gave Larry a nod of thanks and hurried back outside.

Running the gauntlet once more, he sidled through the alley to arrive on Higher Market Street and turned right. Back among the bustling crowd of the festival and thankful to be able to mingle and hide, he pushed on, heading for Stacey's shop.

He had a question for her.

When five paces later, a hand grabbed his arm and something as hard as steel dug into his kidney, he had no choice other than to freeze.

Turning toward the figure pressed against his left side, it came as no shock to find Tanya looking up at him.

Tanya

“Hello, Albert. Fancy meeting you here,” she sneered cruelly, jabbing the gun she held just a little deeper into his flesh.

Albert grunted against the pain, but made no attempt to pull away.

“If you shout for help. If you attempt to get away. If you so much as catch your toe on a cobble and trip, I will shoot you, Albert Smith. I will shoot you and then I’ll fire indiscriminately into the crowd to cover my escape.” Tanya knew Albert’s career history; she knew he wouldn’t endanger anyone to save himself. “The only reason I haven’t shot you already is because my employer would like to talk to you."

"Your employer," Albert rasped the words back at her. "A scumbag criminal with a plan to steal food and kidnap people. Who is he?" Albert phrased the question with a masculine pronoun to see how Tanya would react. Finding out the mastermind's gender wouldn't be much, but it would be a start.

All around them, the happy festival visitors were going about their lives. A lady jostled into them, smiling an apology until she saw the expressions contorting both Tanya and Albert's faces.

When the woman hurried back to her party, Tanya stepped just a little closer to Albert.

"He is someone you will meet very soon, Albert. I'm so glad you don't have that damned dog with you today. Lucky for him really because I have a score to settle."

Albert's heart hammered in his chest. This was it – his worst-case scenario. On the brink of catching them in the act he had come too close, risked too much, and was going to pay the price. Much like Tanya, he was pleased Rex wasn't with him, Albert could only imagine what she might have done to eliminate Rex as a threat before tackling the human side of their team.

"Start walking." Tanya rammed the gun into his kidney again, forcing a gasp of pain to burst from Albert's lips.

"Where are we going?"

She jabbed him again, bruising his insides with the muzzle of her handgun.

"No questions, Albert. You'll get answers soon enough, but they won't do you any good." She fell silent, steering him with the gun and with the vice grip she maintained on the elbow joint of his left arm.

Fifty yards later, she spoke again, this time to ask a question.

"Who are you, Albert? I mean, who do you work for? That's what my boss wants to know. How is it that you keep showing up where we are working?"

Working? Albert thought her choice of phrase was amusing.

With a tired shrug, he admitted, "I'm no one. Just an ex-cop who spotted a clue and chose to follow it."

"Why, Albert? Why get yourself into all this bother? You could have walked away at any time, and we would have let you. But you had to keep on, didn't you? Look at where it got you."

"Someone has to stop you."

Tanya laughed. "And what? You're the right man for the job?"

Albert twisted his head to look around and down at her. "No, but I was the only man in the equation. I had to keep trying to figure out what was going on because no one else would." A new question occurred to him. "Did you kidnap Argyll?"

"Argyll? I don't know who that is … oh, hold on, the kipper smoker?"

"They are haddocks actually, but yes. Did you?"

Tanya smiled at the memory. "Yup," she boasted. "I walked right up behind him in the middle of Arbroath and hit him with a stun gun. Baldwin caught him and into the van he went."

They crossed out of Higher Market Street, turning right onto Buller Street. They were going to pass Stacey's shop if they kept going the way they were. Would she see? Would she call the police? Albert had been doing his best to avoid the authorities since he arrived. Given his current predicament, getting arrested and locked up while they sorted out who was guilty of what, would be a marked improvement.

"Where is Baldwin?" he asked. "Too badly injured to play along after Rex bit him?" Albert put a soupcon of superiority into his tone, aiming to annoy his captor and keep her attention on him lest she see Stacey or Rex looking out from the shop window for his return.

Tanya giggled. "Baldwin is dead." She felt Albert stiffen, and the giggle turned into a laugh. "Don't worry, Albert. He didn't die of his injuries. Not directly anyway. I shot him in the head."

The news, the way she laughed when she said it, silenced Albert and drove home how deeply in trouble he was.

Sounding happy about it, Tanya added, “I’ll probably be doing the same to you this time tomorrow.”

Spreading the Team

Rex stood vigil at the door, looking through the window at the people going by outside. His human had gone off without him. Admittedly, Rex had been separated from the old man several times in the recent weeks, though rarely on purpose.

It was unusual though for Albert to go off without Rex by his side and the dog was finding it most disconcerting.

Stacey had gone to her computer, distracting herself by checking online sales. There were a few which she would package up and send later today or possibly tomorrow, depending on how the day proceeded.

When her phone rang, she almost jumped out of her skin.

The number wasn't one she recognised, and she almost dismissed it with a swipe of her finger before changing her mind.

"Hello?"

"Stacey, it's Terry."

Stacey's free hand formed a fist.

"What do you want, Terry? Isn't it enough that you are working my brother like a slave? His friend died today." She was about to skewer him with questions about whether they were smuggling drugs or something when Terry's reply stopped her dead.

"Where is Rodney?"

She didn't answer for a second and when she did her counter question wasn't the most dazzling.

"What do you mean, where is Rodney? He's in your kitchen making pasties like a slave, same as he is every day."

"Oh, yeah, so he is," sneered Terry sarcastically. "That's why I called the woman in town who hates me more than any other. Look there he is loading pasties into the oven right now. Whoops, no he isn't! He left here half an hour ago and I haven't seen him since. I've got Raven doing his job with Pamela trying to run the shop by herself!"

Stacey tried to make sense of the information. Rodney left her shop more than twenty minutes ago protesting that he had to get back to work. If he wasn't there, then were did he go?

"I … I need to call him," she blurted, her thumb moving to end the call with Terry.

"Don't bother," Terry shouted, "he's not answering the phone. On second thoughts, do bother. Please. Maybe he'll answer for you. If you get him, ask if he's seen Cody."

"Cody is missing too?"

"Been gone for hours," shouted Terry. "I'd sack the pair of them if I cou …." The line went dead halfway through his final sentence, Stacey cutting him off. Terry glared at his phone until a shout from Raven sent him running to one of the ovens where the latest batch of pasties were starting to smoke.

In her shop, Stacey thumbed Rodney's name in her recently dialled list. Her pulse was banging, making her feel anxious and lightheaded.

It went to voicemail, and she tried again with the same result. Her feet twitched with indecision. What should she do? It was exactly what Albert said only sooner than he predicted. Cody and Rodney were missing. Had they been kidnapped already?

She wanted to call Albert, but didn't have a number for him. At no point today had it occurred to her to take it.

Should she call the police? Was it time? Her finger hovered over the keypad ready to start hitting the number nine.

What would she tell them? Albert's question echoed in her head.

Stuffing the phone back into her pocket, Stacey went to the front door where she had to lean over Rex to get to the lock. With a yank to make sure it wasn't going to open, she said, "Sorry, Rex, I need to go out. You stay here, okay? Albert will be back soon, I'm sure. I know he can't get in, but I won't be long."

Rex twisted around to track the woman as she headed for the door that led through to the back of the shop.

"Hold on. Where are you going?" Stacey was the second person in the last thirty minutes to tell Rex they wouldn't be long. Time meant very little to Rex much like any other dog. The sun came up, the sun went down, there were times for eating ... well, okay, every time was for eating if the chance arose, but the point is, when it came to people, 'I won't be long' meant nothing. All a dog knows is that the person is gone.

Stacey ran out the door which shut behind her and left the building using the fire exit a previous tenant had installed many years ago in line with building regs.

She was heading for the quayside where Cody kept his boat. She had no idea if finding it there or discovering it was missing would be better, but it was a starting place.

Hurrying, she dialled Rodney's number again and placed the phone to her ear.

Back in the shop, Rex frowned at the door. Not the front door, but the inner one which led to the back of the shop. Stacey had left the building; his nose assured him of that, and the fresh scent that blew in from outside told him there was another way out.

His human was out there somewhere, and recent history dictated that he was probably in trouble. Nudging the inner door open with his face, Rex followed his nose toward the smell of outside. It led him to a small gap beneath a door.

A fire door.

One with a bar in the middle designed to facilitate easy egress in an emergency.

He would have smiled like the Grinch if he knew how.

Once outside, Rex lifted his nose to the sky and drew in a deep breath. He could find no trace of his human's odour, and now on the wrong side of the building knew that he had to go all the way around to get to where he last saw the old man.

Setting off, he picked up another smell and chose to follow that.

Out of the Frying Pan

Just as Rex set off, Albert drew level with the front of Stacey's fancy dress shop. He could see inside, but only glanced, worried a stare might drew Tanya's attention that way in time for Rex to appear. It was one thing to find himself in dire straits, another entirely if Rex was involved.

For ten minutes, he'd been trying to figure out what he could do to break her hold or do something that might allow him to escape without endangering anyone else. They were heading out of the town's central business district and would shortly be able to see the old stone bridge that linked the two halves of the ancient seaside resort.

Where they were going, Tanya refused to reveal, but Albert knew for certain that before they were away from the crowds, he was going to have to make a move. If he allowed Tanya to trap him in a vehicle or render him unconscious, he would stay that way until he got to wherever they wanted him to go.

Then it would be too late.

Sure he wanted to know who was behind it, but Albert would be content to read about it in the paper after he'd delivered the police the evidence they needed to begin an investigation of their own.

He had no desire to meet the Gastrothief in person.

"Mr Smith!" Albert spasmed at the sound of his name. "I say, Mr Smith. Albert Smith." He already knew whose voice was raised to be heard above the crowd. It was coming from dead ahead, and as the crowd moved, it parted slightly to give Albert a clear view of Superintendent Charters.

She was smiling and had her hand raised above her head to catch his attention.

Albert heard Tanya swear, winced when he felt the gun dig into his back again, then with a shove that made him stumble, his would-be kidnapper was gone.

Albert regained control of his feet and spun around to see where she had gone.

Tanya was nowhere in sight.

A wave of relief washed through him, leaving a weightless, dizzy feeling in its wake. He got no recovery time though because Superintendent Charters was upon him.

Albert mumbled, “Out of the frying pan …” and turned to face her. Should he raise his hands, wrists together and ready for the cuffs? He couldn’t decide. She had to be calling his name because she knew who he was now.

“Mr Smith, are you all right? You look ever so pale.”

Unable to believe his luck, Albert forced his face to keep up with the changing emotions. She clearly didn't know who he was yet, or she would be calling for assistance and manhandling him.

"A touch too much of the cider," Albert latched onto a believable lie. "How is the festival going? Much in the way of petty crime?"

"A few thefts. A brief panic over a missing child. The usual sort of thing. And there is a pickpocket operating in town. We had a bunch of calls about missing wallets and purses this morning. Oddly there's been nothing in the last hour. It's almost as if the miscreant behind it chose to call it quits."

Albert did his best to keep his face from reacting. He wanted to leave the area, and to collect Rex – if Tanya came back, she was going to get bitten.

Getting his feet moving, he started in the direction the superintendent had been walking. "I heard there was a body found on the beach this morning. Nothing suspicious, I hope."

Superintendent Charters seemed to notice the absence of Albert's dog for the first time.

Frowning slightly, she said, "I'm afraid I can't talk about that other than to confirm there was a body. It was found by a man out walking his dog. A large German Shepherd."

Albert remarked, “Plenty of those about.”

“Yes,” replied the superintendent, drawling the word a little as she considered it. “Well, the gentleman in question has vanished, which is a little odd, but I’m sure such things happened in your day just as they do now.”

“Well,” said Albert, pausing in the street when they drew level with the fancy dress shop. “I think I ought to take a rest. Maybe let the cider work its way from my system. Good luck with all the policing.”

He bade Superintendent Charters a good day and reversed his course toward Stacey’s place.

She watched him go, saw when he tried the door to the shop and found it wouldn't open. There was something niggling in her head, but with no idea why and with a dozen other things to occupy her thoughts, she angled her feet back toward the seafront and continued on her way.

Less than a minute later, the voice of Sergeant Andrews came over her radio.

"Ma'am, I have an update for you on this morning's murder victim and you are not going to believe it."

Superintendent Charters encouraged her sergeant to continue.

"It's the man who found the body, Ma'am. He gave a false name."

"Yes, you told me that earlier."

“Well, Thorpe just caught up with the landlord of the bed and breakfast. The man staying there was registered under the right name: Roy Hope, but he matches the description of the old man we met last night.”

“Albert Smith?” Superintendent Charter’s eyebrow furrowed.

“Yes, Ma’am. There’s a warrant out for his arrest! He’s the one behind that explosion in Kent two nights ago!”

Busted

Rex clearly wasn't inside the shop and there was no sign of Stacey either. Thumping on the doorframe with a frustrated fist, Albert grimaced and questioned what to do.

He needed a sit down. His left kidney felt positively bruised. Puffing out his cheeks, he chose to get off the street. He believed it was entirely too possible that Tanya was still watching him.

Walking away, he ducked down the first alley he came to, passing between a sandwich shop and a public house to arrive on Quay Street. The river ran by on the other side of the street, which was more a tarmac apron between the outer row of businesses and the water than it was a road.

Stopping to get his bearings and question which way he ought to go, Albert admitted to himself that he needed a minute. The pain in his side could not be ignored and perhaps staying close to the shop was the right thing to do.

He didn't have Stacey's number, a massive oversight on his part he now realised, but rather than fear the worst, he told himself she might have just taken the dog for a walk. In all the excitement, Albert hadn't given one thought to his dog's bathroom requirements.

Begrudgingly accepting his limitations, Albert tracked back to the pub and stepped inside just in time for Superintendent Charters to miss seeing him leave the street.

He didn't see her either, his eyes fixed on a comfortable looking chair near the windows that looked out over Fore Street.

A swift visit to the bar got him a stiff whisky, a drink he never imbibed but one he believed would take the edge off the pain in his lower back, and a pint of cider which he got because he was in the West Country and had a worrying suspicion it might be his last for a while.

His bottom had just about made contact with the seat of the chair when half a dozen police officers ran past the window. His pint glass stopped moving an inch from his lips, his eyes wide as he watched Superintendent Charters come back into view.

The senior police officer was barking orders. He couldn't hear what she was saying, not through the wall of the pub and with the background conversation around him, but even though he couldn't lip read, he knew his name when she said it.

He was busted.

The pint glass wobbled rather more than he would have liked to admit as he carried it the remaining distance to his mouth. Albert would recall later that he couldn't remember drinking the pint in one go, but when he placed it back down on the table, the glass was empty.

It was a disappointing end to his adventure and was coming just when he thought he had the Gastrothief in his sights. It wasn't so much the embarrassment that would come to his children, though that did bother him, it was the doubt. People doubted him. They didn't believe him. He was right and he'd been singularly unable to prove it.

That could have changed tonight. And now it wouldn't.

Albert picked up the tumbler of whisky and swirled the honey-coloured liquid around, watching it as he contemplated life and waited for the police to come into the pub.

Sighing, he wished Rex was at his side.

Something in the Water

Rex arrived at the quayside where he found the scent trail ended. Upon exiting the rear of Stacey's shop, it took only seconds for his nose to find a smell he knew: that of the man whose scent was on the dead man's clothes.

There was no trace of Albert's scent and leaving by the back door made the orientation of the buildings confusing. Given the chance, Rex would have made his way around to the front of Stacey's shop to then set off in the direction he last saw his human heading.

However, now he had a different scent to follow and wondered if perhaps he ought to just see if he could figure out who killed the man on the beach.

The trail led him along the quayside and away from the glut of people in the town centre. It took Rex more than a minute to figure out that he was following two trails. Because there were so many human scents around and they were mixed with a plethora of other odours including a powerful stench drifting along the river from the fish market, he at first assumed the second human male smell was simply heading in the same direction.

It wasn't though and Rex knew the person this scent belonged to as well – Stacey's brother. He was with the man whose scent was on the dead man's clothes. Rex kept his nose going, pausing every now and then to confirm he was still on the right track.

If the two men were together, were they both somehow involved in the murder of the man on the beach? Rex had no wish to jump to conclusions, but they were definitely going to the same place at the same time and both scents bore the markers of working in the pasty shop.

Rex followed the scents until he came to the end of the quayside. There were humans around, though not very many. It was cooler here, exposed to the on-shore breeze that ruffled his fur coat continually. The people were gathered in the streets of the town, away from the beach and the water.

Observing the chop of the waves, greatly increased from this morning, Rex reached an unavoidable conclusion: the trail had gone dead.

Standing on the concrete at the edge of the quay, he sniffed at the air. The men had gone and there was only one conclusion Rex could draw: they had stepped off the quayside and onto a boat. It was that or they had dived into the sea which Rex thought distinctly less likely.

Disappointed, Rex was turning away when a forlorn sound reached his ears. It was curious enough to make him turn back. Staring in the direction it had come from, he could see nothing. More used to relying on his nose for information, Rex knew his powerful olfactory system wasn't going to deliver an answer on this occasion – the sea had a way of smothering scents.

Listening for the sound to be repeated, Rex was just turning away for a second time when he heard it again.

It was animal in origin, Rex felt certain, and it wasn't human.

Staring across the mouth of the river as it met the sea, his eyes narrowed on a spot near the rocky shore on the other side. Had he seen something move?

He moved forward and in so doing almost lost his leading foot over the edge of the quayside. With a step back to be sure he was on solid ground, Rex was looking the right way when the sound came again and this time he saw a flipper when it arced above the surface of the water.

It was a seal.

Unsure as to what he was seeing, Rex barked, “Hey!”

The only answer it returned was the same pathetic, forlorn wail.

However, as Rex stared and questioned if the seal might be playing a trick on him, another popped up right beneath Rex’s chin.

Bobbing up from the surface of the waves, it surprised Rex, making him dance back a yard before advancing to look over the edge again.

"Come to warn me to stay on the shore again, have you?" Rex growled, glancing down at the seal with a surly expression. It was some kind of trick – one seal making him look so the other could make him jump. They were probably going to laugh about it together and tell their friends.

Rex wasn't expecting the seal's response.

"It's Gus! He's trapped!" Barked the seal. "I can't get him out!"

Rex narrowed his eyes.

"Trapped, eh? In the water. I bet that happens a lot. What's the ploy? Convince me to dive in to help?"

Leaving the quayside without a second glance at the seal, Rex's paws froze when the seal barked again.

"Pleaaaaasse!"

The cry for help carried a depth of emotion Rex could not ignore. Angry with himself, he twisted around to look into the seal's eyes.

"He's stuck in a piece of old fishing net," the seal revealed. "It's wedged in some rocks and Gus can't get free. Plus, the tide is coming in. He's going to drown!"

Rex frowned. "Drown? How can a seal drown?"

"We're not fish! We hold our breath just like other mammals."

This was big news to Rex who thought all creatures in the sea could breathe underwater.

Looking across the water to the seal's friend, Rex heard the forlorn sound Gus was making and now it made sense. He was in the same spot, and though Rex could not be sure, when the waves shifted, he thought he saw something blue – the fishing net.

Huffing out an annoyed breath, Rex really didn't want to help, but accepted his nature for what it was. If he walked away, it would plague him for weeks.

Spinning around to face inland, he began barking.

“Hey! Hey, humans! There is a seal in trouble. I know you all love this stuff. Get over here and help me!”

The frenzied barking caught the attention of more than two dozen people, all of whom were within a short radius of his location. At first he thought they were all going to ignore him and indeed most did, however, one couple came to check on him.

“Good,” Rex barked and spun on the spot when they came near. “Well volunteered. Now you need a boat or something.”

“What’s he barking about?” asked Beryl, aiming the question at her husband, Alf.

“How am I supposed to know, love?”

They had enjoyed the company of dogs themselves during their forty-six years of marriage but were without one now having lost their beloved Springer Spaniel in the spring.

"Oh, look, there's a seal," Beryl observed, pleased to spot the wild animal up close as it was.

"I guess that's what he was barking at then."

"No, no, no!" Rex barked, aiming his nose across the water. "You have to look over there. There's a seal stuck in a fishing net."

Alf gave the German Shepherd a pat on his shoulder.

"Where do you suppose this fellow's owner is?"

Beryl looked around.

"Well, there's no one in sight, is there? Maybe he got lost."

Alf focused on the dog.

"He's staring out to sea. Maybe his owner went on a boat trip and left this chap tied up somewhere only he got free."

"That makes sense," Beryl agreed.

The seal asked, "How come you dogs always hang around with humans? Don't you get frustrated by their absolute stupidity?"

Rex had no response to give and was too busy trying to figure out relative velocities, tide strengths, and other factors.

He had a plan. It wasn't one he liked, but no options were presenting themselves.

Alf took hold of Rex's collar.

"I guess we ought to call the police and have this chap taken somewhere safe. It wouldn't be right to just leave him here."

Beryl nodded her head, reaching into her handbag to find her phone.

Neither expected what happened next.

In a burst of motion, Rex bucked and twisted, throwing Alf's half hearted grip loose. The human cursed and yowled as his shoulder joint took a yank, but Rex didn't look back.

A small fishing vessel was on its way back to the quayside, and Rex was willing to bet they would change course to fish him out of the water. Or rather, as he launched himself over the seal's head, he prayed that would be the case because there was no way back onto land now without a jolly good swim.

Animal Hero

The cold bite of the water gripped Rex's skin and the salt stung at his nose. The rushing tide had lifted the sea so the drop to the surface was less than four feet, but gravity still pulled him under the surface.

Watching from the quayside, their disbelieving eyes fixed on the spot where the dog vanished beneath the dark waves, Beryl and Alf breathed a sigh of relief when he popped back up a moment later.

Sucking in a breath, and paddling with all his might, Rex struck out for the far shore. It hadn't looked as far when he was still on land. Now, at sea level, with the waves constantly jostling him to steal his view only to return it a moment later, Rex questioned if this had been such a bright idea.

"Is that as fast as you can go?" asked Robbie, circling back. Upon seeing the dog launch himself into the water, he'd kicked for the far shore and was halfway there when he turned to spot Rex barely three yards from the quayside.

Rex's jowls flapped as he sucked in some air and spat, "Yes! When this is done perhaps you and I should have a race on land."

Robbie acknowledged, "Fair point."

Gus's forlorn cry for help echoed across the water and this time, forced to question what the dog was doing, Beryl and Alf heard it.

"What is that?" asked Alf, squinting at something blue. It had only been there for a second between the waves, and he might have ignored it had the strange animal in distress sound not come from the same direction.

"You know," Beryl strained her eyes. "I think that might be a seal."

Armed with new information, Alf needed only a second to assess what he was seeing. There was no question the German Shepherd was heading directly for the seal on the far bank. Or rather, he was trying to. The tide, flowing into the mouth of the river, was pushing Rex off course. For every yard he went forward, he had to swim three just to stay on target.

Robbie tolerated it for a while, but it was all just too slow.

"Here, hold still," he honked in Rex's ear. "I'm going to give you a tow."

Rex got no say in the matter, and his protests were cut off when the seal bit hold of his collar and trebled his speed. Now cutting through the surf, Rex couldn't speak for fear of drowning, and he was going sideways with half his face in the water.

What he needed to develop, Rex thought in between panicked breaths, was the ability to take a breath through his left ear.

Barking and almost getting a lungful of sea water, Rex shouted, "Stop!"

They were three quarters of the way across the river mouth and thus less than twenty yards from the trapped seal. It was close enough and the fishing vessel was bearing down on them. It would pass them to port, heading down the centre of the river and Rex was certain it could not fail to see him in the water.

For good measure, he started barking as he paddled against the tide.

"Hey! Hey, humans! Over here!"

Robbie joined in, adding his voice in an act that would bewilder locals and be discussed for years to come.

In the wheelhouse of the little fishing boat, John Marcone blinked and rubbed his eyes. For thirty-six years he'd been fishing the waters off Looe and never once had he seen anything so bizarre. Leaning out of his side window, he called to the two men on deck.

"Here, fellas. You need to take a look at this."

He cut the engine, then chunked the gearbox into reverse, edging the throttle until the boat was holding against the tide.

Off their starboard side, a large dog and a seal bobbed in the waves, barking furiously and when he went to look, both turned tail and set out for the shore, barking and honking as they went.

“That was bizarre,” remarked, John’s son, Leslie. “I ain’t never heard of no seal playing in the water with a dog before.”

“I guess it must be theirs,” said Tommy, the third hand, lighting a cigarette and nodding his head at an elderly couple on the quayside.

“Can you make out what they are saying?” asked John, straining to hear their words against the onshore breeze.

Both Beryl and Alf were pointing and gesticulating, not to mention arguing about what the international sign for ‘trapped seal’ might be. Alf puffed out his cheeks, tucked his elbows into his sides and clapped his hands together while barking like a seal.

While there could be no doubt as to what animal he was attempting to imitate, the crew of the fishing vessel had no idea what his next set of actions were supposed to mean.

“What are you doing?” asked Beryl, staring down at her husband where he lay now on the concrete of the quayside, acting like a seal trapped in a net.

“I’m being a seal trapped in a net,” he huffed, annoyed that he needed to point out the obvious.

“Do you think he’s all right?” asked Leslie. “Is he having a seizure?”

John scrunched up his face, trying to decide whether he ought to just carry on and land their catch. Swinging around to check on the dog – he liked dogs and was concerned the animal was in more danger than anyone realised. The tide was almost in and would soon reverse. There was a rip tide just off shore that would carry him a mile out at least.

It was then that he spotted a seal. The waves dropped for a split second, revealing a face pressed tight against the blue nylon mesh of a net.

He swore, and ran back to the wheelhouse, leaving his son and Tommy wondering what they had missed.

Coaxing the boat across the river mouth, and taking care of the rocks on the far bank, they didn't have to get much closer to see precisely why the dog and seal had been making so much noise.

Rex reached the rocks on the far shore and scrambled, bedraggled from the sea. Water streamed from his coat, but there was no time to shake out the excess.

Exiting the water ten yards upstream from Gus, Rex was forced to negotiate the tricky rocks to get to him. Robbie was already there, bobbing in the water just a yard from his friend.

From there the seal gave encouragement.

"Just hold on, Gus. The humans are coming. They'll get you free."

It was completely unnatural for the seals to let the humans come anywhere near them. For sure they got close sometimes when the odd two-legged creatures went diving off the coast, but that was just curiosity and playfulness. Now they had to embrace the fish stealers' presence and hope they had a way to free Gus before the tide rose any further.

Rex came down the rocks until his paws were back in the water. Wading out to chest height, his front foot slipped into nothingness again when he encountered the drop off, only this time he didn't fall in.

"You brought the dog?" questioned Gus. He wanted to say something rotten, but his energy had been sapped by fighting to get free.

'And he brought the humans," replied Robbie.

Choosing to ignore Gus's tone, Rex ducked his head beneath the waves to bite hold of the net.

Could he bite through it?

It took no time at all to confirm he was never going to win that battle, but it was okay because the humans really were arriving.

Getting the boat as close as he dared, John shouted for Leslie to help Tommy balance. Timing the swell, and with a pocketknife between his lips, the third hand whispered a prayer and leapt.

His timing wasn't great, but the confluence of factors to calculate were many and unpredictable. The boat shifted as he pushed off, dropping a yard and making the gap bigger. Mercifully, Tommy found rock beneath his feet when he landed even if it was several feet beneath the waves.

The sea might be at its warmest, but the cold water that swept up on the next wave to gently kiss the underside of Tommy's nether region made him gasp several curse words, nevertheless.

Forging through the water and gripping the rocks to keep him from going for a swim if he lost his footing, he approached the trapped seal.

A small crowd had gathered on the quayside. Drawn by Alf and Beryl's shouts, many were filming the event. More were watching from the other shore where the road climbed steeply to Hannafore Point. Spotting the unfolding drama, a couple in town for the festival had pulled over to get a better look. There wasn't really room to stop at the side of the road and the resulting traffic trying to get around them had caused a tail-back that now had no interest in going anywhere.

In the water, Gus understood that the human was coming to help him, and that he couldn't free himself, but a life of living wild generated an impulse reaction. Bucking and barking, he threatened the man.

Nearly there, Tommy twitched his eyes to look at the dog. Rex was standing vigil, unable to do more than he already had.

"Go on then," Rex encouraged. "Cut the net. There's a good boy."

The dog was calm and friendly. Why wasn't the seal? He was here to help it. Showing both hands, even though one held a knife, Tommy covered the final feet at snail's pace.

The seal continued to buck and writhe to a chorus of 'Oohs' and 'Ahhhs' from the onlookers.

The net holding the seal in place was below the surface, stretched taut by the animal inside as it fought to stay above the waves.

Tommy tried to grab the nylon rope, hoping he could cut through it quickly, but Gus snapped at him, causing his rescuer to fall backward into the waves.

Now soaked to his nipples, Tommy was impressed to have kept hold of the knife. Unfortunately, the onlookers were now laughing, entertained by his antics which, quite frankly, he thought were nothing short of heroic.

With that in mind, he gathered himself, surged from the water, grabbed the blue nylon and held on tight. The knife was sharp, but still took effort and several seconds to make the cut. A second cut and then a third, freed the seal who, with a thrash of his body, vanished beneath the dark waves.

A cheer erupted along with applause. All for the human, Rex noted, who was waving to the crowd on both sides of the river like a gold medallist on a victory lap.

The job was done and the number of people taking pictures or filming guaranteed Tommy a spot in the local paper. The downside was the likelihood that he would be forced to buy a round at his local when they put the pictures on the wall, but perhaps his new fame would finally be enough to convince Sadie Black to go out with him.

Cheered by that thought, Tommy started to clamber up the rocks.

Rex watched the water until Gus's head reappeared. Whoops of joy followed, the humans loving the happy ending. Rex got a tired nod from the seal and another from Robbie as they vanished under the surface again.

How long had elapsed while he was playing animal hero? Rex knew it was distinctly longer than he wanted and now he was on the wrong side of the river. The swim had made him feel tired – a snack was in order, but his own human was not around to supply it and Albert was just as likely to be in trouble as he was when Rex originally left Stacey's shop.

Following Tommy's path up the rocks, Rex steered his way around the humans and set off for the bridge. Just to get back to his start point he had maybe two miles to go on fatigued limbs. To make it worse he was both soaking wet and getting cold.

With a shake to rid his coat of as much water as possible, he started walking.

A New Disguise

Albert's whisky stayed in the glass for more than an hour. An hour in which he'd been waiting for the cops to find him. Sitting in his chair looking out over the streets of Looe, Albert had a scene in his head.

The cops would enter the establishment – just a couple of them. Spotting their suspect sitting quietly by himself, they would be wary enough to call for back up, waiting just out of sight though forgetting Albert would hear their radios. Back-up would come, perhaps in the guise of someone more senior and they would quietly encourage patrons to leave the bar. Overly cautious in case the suspected terrorist was armed, the senior person – possibly Superintendent Charters herself, would address him.

At that point, and without once looking their way, Albert planned to slowly lift the whisky to his lips and down it in one. The scenario had a certain … Clint Eastwoodness to it. All he needed was a poncho and a hat. And perhaps a squint.

However, the scene remained unplayed, the cops fanning out to quietly lock down the town and never once setting foot inside the pub in which their suspect sat.

It left Albert with a dilemma: what to do?

As it stood, he was free to pursue his investigation still. That meant there remained a chance he could catch Tanya and her friends in the act. The police were all over the town which worked in his favour when it came time to arrest them, but in his opinion it also made it less likely the Gastrothief's agents would pursue their target.

Whatever he did, there was no way he could stay dressed as he was. Superintendent Charters would have been accurate in her description of his outfit and appearance.

He was going to have to change it.

Could he get into Stacey's shop? Was she there? The front door was locked, he knew that much. However, given how deeply in the doodoo he already found himself, a little recreational breaking and entering wasn't going to matter.

He downed the whiskey with just a tinge of disappointment that he didn't get to act out the scene in his head. Taking his glasses to the bar, Albert ducked his head to look for cops outside the windows. Seeing none, he dipped his head at the landlord and walked out into the street.

The sun had made its way toward the horizon, taking the light with it. It wasn't fully dark yet, but Albert knew twilight had only half an hour left in it at most.

Hoping Stacey might prove to be in the shop now, Albert was heading for Fore Street when he spotted a door hanging slightly ajar. Craning his neck to look and questioning his own assessment twice, he was certain the door had to lead into the back of her shop. It was a fire exit, he discovered, levering it open with his fingertips. He had no idea how it came to be left that way and didn't care. A sigh of relief to be out of sight was instantly pushed to the side – he needed to get on with the task in hand.

"Rex? Stacey?"

No response came, it was disappointing, yet he assumed they were together wherever they were.

"They're probably out looking for you," he remarked to himself as he made his way from the back rooms into the front of Stacey's shop.

Hanging on the racks he found a fine array of clothing to pick from. None of it was suitable though. Dressing as a clown was out. Tanya would spot the disguise for sure this time and the moment she questioned why she was seeing it again, she would see through the make-up.

No, he needed something different. Something that disguised his face.

Selecting a spaceman outfit, he picked up the helmet. It sort of did the trick, but with the visor down it was hard to see and with it up his face was exposed. Also, he had no peripheral vision.

Placing the helmet back on the shelf, he slid hanger after hanger from left to right, considering and discarding each choice until an idea jumped out at him.

Going back to the second costume on the rack, Albert held it up. It came with a bowler hat. That did nothing to hide his face, but twisting slowly around to aim his eyes at Stacey's make up box once more, a grin spread across his face.

Just Don't Move

It took fifteen minutes for Albert to decide he was happy with the effect he wanted to achieve. It was far from perfect, but it was most definitely the best he could do and with the sun already gone from the sky he could only assume his chance to catch the Gastrothief's agents was imminent. They might not strike for an hour or even a couple of hours, but if they were going to act, it would be soon.

He needed to be in place and ready.

Aiming his eyes to the street outside, he would have spat out his false teeth if he had any. Tanya's friends, the man and the woman, were walking past the front windows.

He ran to the front door intending to follow only to find one needed a key to open it. Cursing, Albert ran as fast as he could to get to the fire exit at the back. He made sure to close it behind him, then darted around the buildings to exit onto Fore Street via an alleyway some forty yards up the road.

Looking around for his quarry, his heart chose to stop when he saw them coming straight for him. Blind panic that he'd already blown it faded quickly when he remembered he was in disguise.

His disguise, however, called for an absolute lack of motion. Assuming a pose he hoped he could hold, Albert backed against a wall and froze.

"Oh, look, George, it's one of those living statues. Those people are ever so clever the way they don't move at all for hours at a time."

Albert tried not to move his eyes to see who was talking.

A couple in their sixties stopped right in front of him, the man jovially waving a hand in front of Albert's face to see if he could convince the statue to blink.

"You need a cap or a pot or something," the lady advised, fishing around in her purse for some coins. "I'll just pop them here," she smiled, dropping some loose change into his left breast pocket.

Tanya's colleagues walked by, continuing down the street.

The couple moved on, leaving Albert to watch his quarry.

"Urrr, look, Bob, it's one of those stupid living statues," remarked a teenage boy, elbowing his friend. "I bet I can make it move." The kid was about to show off to his pals, of which there were quite a few, when Albert decided his target was far enough away.

The kid was about to kick Albert in the shin and jumped half out of his skin when the statue abruptly moved.

Sidestepping the kick, Albert shoved against the kid's shoulder, knocking him over to a roar of laughter from his friends.

Getting looks from those in his immediate vicinity, Albert hurried onward. The disguise was working, that was the good news. The idea had come to him in a flash of inspiration. He needed something that would hide his face, but he didn't want to wear a mask because the police and probably Tanya would see it and be suspicious.

However, a living statue at a festival where there were thousands of people – that wasn't suspicious at all. He could freeze if he needed to, and the police would walk straight by.

In all honesty, he was nowhere near confident it would work and hoped he didn't have to find out.

Tanya's colleagues were a few yards ahead of him; just far enough that he could keep them in sight. He was going to pull it off, that's what Albert told himself over and over as he made his way through the town. They were waiting for the evenings festivities to kick off and for the winner of the cider competition to be announced. That would trigger their plan he hoped. All he had to do was follow, stay out of sight, and wait. When they made their move, he would call the police.

Provided the police didn't spot him beforehand, it was fool proof.

Or, it might have been, if Albert hadn't missed one vital element.

Cody.

Close the Shop

Cody was confident Rodney had told him everything. It wasn't as if he had given the idiot any choice. Stacey knew about the royal engagement, but not about Cody's plan for it if Rodney was to be believed. And Cody did believe him.

He would deal with Stacey later, that would be easy enough if a little messy and unfortunate, but it was the old man who was most bothering Cody.

Rodney had no idea who he was. According to Rodney the man had lots of questions about the pasty shop and a wild story about someone wanting to kidnap the people working there. It was obviously utter rubbish though Cody could not see what was driving the old man to make up such a daft story.

Too old to be anything to do with the police … too old to be anything much at all in Cody's opinion, the old man was bizarrely dressed as a living statue now, his face made up to match his clothing, so it all blended into one.

Yet more bizarre was the old man's behaviour. Cody had been watching the front of the shop for Stacey to return when he saw the old man inside. With no sign of the shopkeeper, Cody observed the old man changing his outfit and donning makeup before rushing through the door that led to the back of the shop.

At the time, Cody had twitched, trying to decide what to do, and when the old man appeared further down the street, he chose to follow. Stacey could wait. If his plan for the royal family were known to the man inside the living statue costume, whoever he was, then Cody needed to know how and who else knew. And what the old man was up to.

Strutting down the road, not bothering to close the distance because the old man's choice of clothing made him easy to track, Cody thought about what he wanted to do.

There was a unique opportunity to get what he wanted - to strike at the royals and score one for the common people. His need to protect the plan was paramount and that meant dealing with the old man just as he had with Rodney.

The others had to be involved though. They had to understand the stakes.

Taking out his phone, Cody called Terry.

"Cody! Cody where the heck have you been all day? We have been swamped ..."

Cody's bark cut Terry off. "Shut up! While you've been making pasties, I've been protecting us. We have a leak. A traitor in our midst. Did you know that?"

Terry's anger toward Cody took a back seat, pushed out of the way by fear and anxiety.

"What? What do you mean? No one would say anything."

"Rodney did," Cody spat, his eyes never leaving the back of the old man's head. "Rodney told his sister and now there's some old man poking around asking questions."

Terry's head spun and panic gripped his insides.

"An old man? The one from the shop this morning? The one in the clown suit? Who is he?"

"That's what we're about to find out."

"We … no, Cody, there are customers in the shop. I can't just …"

"You can and you will. Close the shop, Terry. Kick the last of the customers out with free pasties. I don't care. Everything we have talked about. Everything we have hoped and planned for is about to unravel. I'm going to my uncle's boat shed. Meet me there in ten minutes. Bring Raven."

Terry wanted to argue. He also wanted to throw up. A glance showed him how many customers were lined up waiting to be served. Today had been impossible and in some ways he was glad Cody wasn't giving him a choice about closing for the day.

"Terry," Cody warned when the pasty shop owner didn't reply.

A shudder ran through Terry, making him feel weak. Cody was right – they had been talking about taking down the royals since they were in their teens. Since Cody's dad lost his 'By Royal Appointment' title and consequently his business. Cody's dad had never been the same afterward and drank himself to death in less than five years.

But it wasn't for Cody that Terry wanted to attack the monarchy, he truly believed their continued existence and privilege was an outrage the British public should fight to end. He, just as much as Cody, wanted to stage an uprising. The French Revolution, that was their model. March them up to their own executions and dance as a new era of prosperity and equality dawned.

Gripping his phone tightly, he said, "I'm on my way."

Pawn takes Knight

The sharp point of the knife in his back came as a shock, but not nearly so much as the person holding it.

"Who are you?" Albert wanted to know.

He'd been attempting to sidestep the young man in one of those 'oops' moments when two people coming toward one another both go the same way when trying to avoid the other. Inevitably, they bumped, and it was then that Albert discovered the man had been on a deliberate collision course.

The knife, held invisibly inside the young man's jacket sleeve, popped out only when they touched. The man's other hand became a vice grip on Albert's right bicep.

Leaning to get close to Albert, Cody growled, "I'm the fella who'll gut you if you don't do as I say."

Able to look over the top of the man's head, Albert searched for Tanya assuming his latest assailant was the fourth member of her team.

They were near the end of Higher Market Street once more, and right by the alley that led through to the Cliff View Hotel.

"Move," Cody shoved with the knife, driving it into Albert's flesh.

Albert winced, moving because he had no choice as he desperately searched the crowd going by. He could shout for the police right now. He was being held at knifepoint by one of the Gastrothief's agents and he knew where they were staying. If ever there was a time to blow the lid, it was now.

Forced down the narrow alley, he sucked in a breath to shout for help.

Cody released Albert's arm, swinging his hand back to then drive a punch to the old man's gut. He watched with satisfaction when the living statue doubled over coughing and wheezing.

Digging into Albert's shoulder with his fingers, Cody forced Albert to stand upright.

"Try to shout again and I'll stab you. It's time for you to answer some questions."

Struggling for breath, Albert was powerless to resist the younger, stronger man. With the blade digging painfully into his back and a hand that felt like steel guiding him past the hotel, he questioned how it could be that there was no one around.

When he came to the hotel earlier, there were people in the street outside and guests of the hotel coming and going. Right now there was no one.

However, that didn't mean that his passage went unnoticed.

Inside the hotel, Tanya narrowed her eyes at the two men going by. The living statue was in pain, and though it was hard to see his face in the fading light, Tanya's brain convinced her she was seeing Albert Smith.

He was the right height and the right shape. She couldn't explain the costume, but as she thought that, a memory surfaced. There had been a clown this morning. She saw it half a dozen times or more and though she paid it no attention at the time, there had been something familiar about it.

Thinking back now, she cursed herself for not taking a closer look for she was convinced it had been Albert Smith behind the crazy, scary makeup.

Rising from her chair in the window, where she had been waiting for Kelly and Liam to return, she changed her plan. Her colleagues didn't want her help, but she knew Albert was here and that meant trouble. Tanya's plan had been to track and watch her colleagues, expecting to find the old man and his dog snooping and ready to bring the police down on their heads.

However, something else had occurred to interrupt Albert's interference. Tanya had no idea what she was seeing, but the muscular man leading Albert Smith away from town was doing her work for her. She would kill him, whoever he was, and take Albert back to the Gastrothief. There was a fat cheque waiting for her successful return and Tanya had decided that was going to be the end of it.

She could rinse the fat earl for more, but it was all getting a bit too risky. It was time to call it quits.

"One last job," she murmured to herself, taking out her gun and her phone.

Stacey and Rex

Stacey arrived back at her shop flustered, worried, and on the verge of crying. Rodney still wasn't answering his phone which wasn't like him at all. Having set out to look for him and/or Cody, both of whom Terry claimed were missing, she went directly to where she knew Cody kept his boat.

It wasn't there. She'd asked a few of the other fishermen and the people who worked in the shops close to his mooring, but no one could say for sure if they had seen him or Rodney at any point in the last few hours. No one recalled seeing Cody's boat heading out.

Twice she had circumnavigated the centre of town, checking in all her brother's favourite haunts and even calling at his ex-girlfriend's house to see if she knew anything.

There were police everywhere, and when she chose to ask what was happening – just in case it was to do with her brother somehow – she was offered a smile and told they were here to ensure the festival went smoothly. That was all.

It was a lie, and she knew it.

The festival occurred every year and there had never been this many police in Looe before. Hanging around near to them after they told their lies, she heard the name 'Albert Smith' come over the radio.

A jolt of what felt like electricity had shot through her veins. They knew he was here. But what did that mean for her? Had they caught him already? The message had been hard to hear, but it hadn't sounded like that was the case.

Now back at her shop, she unlocked the door and all but fell inside. Was her brother missing or was he just not answering his phone? If he had gone out to sea with Cody, the phone signal might not reach him.

To say she was worried failed to capture the upwelling of emotion crowding her brain, and it was all made worse because choosing to confront Terry directly on her way back to the shop revealed another awful truth – it was closed.

In the height of the festival, with customers raining from the sky, Terry's shop was closed.

Did that mean what she thought it meant? Albert said there were people … the Gastrothief's agents, who were here to target Terry and his staff. Inexplicably, her brother was nowhere to be found and now the shop was shut.

Stacey wanted to check with Albert and longed to have taken his phone number. If the police didn't have him, then maybe it was because he was tracking the kidnappers.

"Come on, Stacey," she raged at herself. "Make a decision." Should she speak to the police? Confess everything. Tell them she was working with Albert Smith? She could lie and say she had no idea who he was at the time, but doubted she could pull it off. They would see through her. But would that matter if ultimately he was innocent? They could catch the people behind the crime and find her brother before … before what? Albert hadn't explained what happened after the Gastrothief's agents took their captives.

Unable to conceive of an alternative, Stacey closed her eyes, accepted her fate, and upon opening them twisted around to face her door. She was going to tell the police everything. It was better than staying quiet and risking her brother's … freedom? Life?

Taking a step forward, she jerked when Rex appeared in the window.

He was outside the front door looking in.

It had taken Rex almost an hour to make his way back to the shop; a long route that took him along one riverbank and over the bridge in three sides of a rectangle that was only a hundred yards if he'd been able to cross the water without needing to go in it again.

His coat has dried on the way so now only the thickest parts were still damp. The exercise had warmed him and dropped street food from the various stalls meant his stomach was no longer empty.

Seeing Stacey coming his way, Rex wagged his tail.

"Where's my human?" he asked the moment she opened the door. He could smell that Albert was not in the shop. His scent lingered, but was not as strong as it would have been if the old man was present.

Stacey, her plan clear in her head, came down to Rex's level.

"Where's Albert?" she asked, ruffling the fur around his neck.

Rex's eyebrows danced.

"You don't know either?" Rex figured the humans were communicating. He saw them fiddling with the strange devices they carried everywhere, and talking into them sometimes. Unable to fully comprehend what a phone did, Rex heard voices of people he knew echoing out from them even though he could never detect their scents.

Twisting around to face down the street, Rex lifted his nose. With a million overlapping odours pinging around his olfactory system, it took a moment to find the smell he wanted.

He set off without a word or a glance in Stacey's direction and the determined gait of his steps made her follow.

"Hey, wait!" she called after the German Shepherd's back end. Almost snapping the key in her haste to lock the door, she had to run to catch up. "Where are you going, Rex? Can you find Albert?"

Rex frowned a little, pausing briefly to test the air.

"If I can find a scent, I can track it. Most dogs can, lady." Confident he had it locked in – it was, after all, a smell he was most familiar with – Rex continued onward along Higher Market Street.

Stacey shot out a hand to grab his collar.

"I'm coming with you," she said, wishing she'd thought to grab his lead from her shop and cursing herself for not wearing better shoes. Admittedly, when she dressed that morning she had no expectation of covering the mileage she had and running had never entered her mind.

Hurrying along at a pace faster than walking, it was a good thing she had hold of Rex because he kept trying to go through dog size gaps and would have lost her in no time had they not been connected.

In the boat shed

Given a rough shove, Albert stumbled, tripped, and fell. He was fortunate that there was a work bench to grab, or he would have landed on the hard floor of the boatshed. His left kidney ached from Tanya's rough treatment, and he could feel where the knife his still unnamed assailant had cut his flesh on the right. The cuts were not bad, but they had leaked, and his shirt was sticking to his skin.

The last thing he needed were more injuries. Assessing his situation, Albert felt certain he was going to have to find an opening and fight to get away. The man with the knife glared at him, the short blade held menacingly in his right hand. He wasn't tall, but he was big. Standing maybe five feet and eight inches, the man compensated for his lack of stature by developing his muscles.

A weapon, Albert thought, something he could swing was what he needed.

Or Rex. Rex would balance the equation.

"Who are you?" the man demanded.

"Just an old man trying to stop a crime from happening." Albert had no idea what was going on, but the fact that his assailant didn't know his name, suggested he wasn't working with Tanya. However, his cryptic answer was precisely the wrong one to give.

Cody moved fast, barrelling forward and swinging a clubbing fist that would have taken Albert to the floor if it had connected.

Scooting around the workbench saved him, but to get to Albert all the man had to do was leap over it.

"What do you know about my operation!" Cody bellowed. "What did that idiot Rodney tell you?"

Albert gripped the bench, ready to use it to throw himself left or right depending on which way the man came.

"I don't know who you are," Albert continued. "I came here to stop a kidnapping and end a crime spree that has been running undetected for months."

"Kidnapping? What on earth are you talking about, old man? You are going to tell me what you know about my plans for the royal family, or I will gut you where you stand."

Albert watched the knife, looking for a tell-tale motion that might tip him off that the man was about to lunge.

"I don't know anything about that," he replied truthfully. "Although ..."

"Yes."

"Well, I know Terry's Pasty Shop has been awarded a contract to supply food to the royal engagement. An engagement no one knows about yet."

The knife rose a foot and Cody's eyes narrowed to an evil squint.

"So there's the truth of it. Did Stacey hire you? Goodness knows that idiot Rodney could never think to do so. Who do you work for?"

Trying to reason with him, Albert said, "I don't work for anyone. My name is Albert Smith. You may have seen me on the news."

The name triggered something. It stopped Cody for a moment while he ran the name through his head.

"Albert Smith," Cody grinned viciously.

"Yes, I'm in a spot of bother with the police. You don't have to fear me. I'm here to help." His words were far from true. He was here to help someone, but the man with the knife wasn't on the list.

Cody brought the knife up and aimed it at Albert.

"You're the terrorist on the news. The one who blew up the oyster beds in Kent." His smile became savage, and he sniggered, "No one is going to miss you."

Albert, rooted to the spot with fear, and silently screaming at himself to start moving, was shocked to see the knife wielder's eyes slowly roll up into his head.

The man crumpled, sinking to his knees and then pitching forward to reveal a person standing behind him holding a piece of wood.

Albert almost said, "Thank you," but his eyes caught up with his brain to deliver a very simple message: Now you are really in trouble.

“Hello again, Albert,” Tanya threw the piece of wood to one side and took out her gun.

Using her left hand, and without taking her eyes off Albert for one moment, she fished in a back pocket to retrieve her phone. She was dressed much as she had been every time Albert had seen her: in tight-fitting jeans, a stretchy top and a sports jacket. The outfit was designed to allow movement and the puffiness of the lightweight coat hid her array of weapons.

With a swish of her hair, she brought the phone up to her ear.

“Kelly, I have Albert Smith.”

Albert listened, making a note of the other woman's name.

"Yes. He was here all along just like I said he would be. I'm taking him back to see the Earl."

Albert's brain seized on the word she used, and he had to fight not to let his face show the emotion he felt. She had to be referring to her boss, the man behind it all. Was he really an Earl? Or was that just a nickname?

"No, you need to come to me. One of the workers from the pasty shop is here."

Albert stayed quiet while Tanya argued, explaining her situation though Albert could only hear her part of it.

"How should I know? He was about to kill Albert, so I don't think they are working together, and I think we can be pretty confident the police are not involved."

Albert took a careful pace to his left. The work bench was devoid of objects he might throw or wield, but the drawers opened on his side. If he could just open them quietly, he might find all manner of treasure inside: A knife to cut through bonds, a screwdriver to use as a stabbing weapon ...

Tanya's gun tracked his movement and blew a hole in the surface of the bench before he'd covered two inches.

"Just giving him a warning," she explained to Kelly. "Look just get down here. I'm in a boat shed down beyond your hotel. Just bring the yacht. You can moor it right outside. There's no one down here but us."

Putting the phone back in her pocket, Tanya lowered her gun, but asked, "Am I going to have to shoot you, Albert? It makes no difference to me. I just need to deliver you still alive. I can do that even with a few holes in you."

"Who's behind this?" Albert asked. "Who pays your wages? What's it all about?"

Tanya smirked. "The end of the world, Albert. The end of the world."

Turning her eyes away, she checked her surroundings.

The man on the floor groaned; he was coming around.

"You know who he is?" she asked.

Albert shook his head. "I thought perhaps he worked with you. You said he was from the pasty shop?" Albert played for time by asking a question he thought Tanya might answer.

He heard her say yacht and one thing he knew about watercraft was how slowly they move. They were going to escape with their victims by sea; a conclusion easily drawn, and he was going to be with them unless he came up with a way to avoid that happening.

Ten minutes ticked by in which Tanya refused to answer any of Albert's questions and promised to shoot him if he asked another.

The sound of voices outside preceded the door to the boat shed swinging inward. Tanya glanced over her shoulder to confirm it was her people arriving.

Albert performed a double take when they came in. Unlike before when they had been dressed much the same as Tanya in casual clothes, they were now dolled up and looking like professional business people.

Kelly especially in a fancy winter coat and sleek boots with matching gloves. Her hair and makeup were flawless – hardly the outfit one would choose for an evening of armed kidnapping.

The man looked at Albert.

“So this is him? What the heck is he wearing?”

"A disguise, dummy," Tanya huffed a laugh at Liam's inability to see the obvious.

Curling his lip, Liam fired back, "He doesn't look like much. How is it that he keeps beating you?"

Tanya quipped, "Don't make me slap you, Liam."

Albert logged another name. Kelly and Liam. The last names he got at the hotel might be accurate, but he doubted it. First names weren't much, but it was more than he had before.

Kelly had chosen to ignore Tanya's prisoner in favour of checking the man on the floor.

"This is Cody Williams," she said with a frown. "What was he doing here?"

Tanya aimed a nod in Albert's direction.

"Ask him."

With three sets of eyes trained in his direction, Albert shrugged.

"I don't know who he is. He grabbed me when I was following you," he nodded at Kelly and Liam.

Liam started forward. "I'll make him tell us."

Tanya grabbed his sleeve.

"There's no time and I don't think he knows. We have to assume he's warned the people at the pasty shop. If this guy works there, you have the pasty maker the Earl wants. His friends will notice he is missing though. Sooner or later, someone is going to sound the alarm. This place is already crawling with police from the body they found this morning."

Albert kept quiet. He didn't need them to know most of the police were in town to catch him.

"Yeah, what was with that anyway," asked Kelly. "The dead guy was one of the ones we were planning to take. Him and the boss of the shop."

Albert couldn't stop the question leaving his lips. "You didn't kill Chris Mason?"

Kelly looked at Albert and then at Liam and Tanya before looking back at the old man.

"Why would we kill him?"

Her answer triggered yet more questions in Albert's head, but he kept them inside – solving a murder was not his priority.

Tanya whacked Liam on his shoulder in a get-on-with-it kind of way.

"You guys had better get moving. Leave the yacht with me. I'll bring it around to the quayside by the fish market when you are ready. There will be no one there at this time of the day. Go grab the cider people ..."

"The winners are not announced for another forty minutes," protested Liam.

Kelly pulled a face at him – he was always feeding Tanya with ammunition to use against them.

"Then we can be ready, can't we?" she snapped.

Liam closed his mouth, glaring at both women.

Heading for the door, Kelly spoke over her shoulder.

"We'll get the pasty makers too." She was making a point. "Cody is the delivery driver." Tanya always came through on her missions and Kelly wasn't going to let her rival be witness to a failure. The operation in Looe had gotten complicated, but that just made it more of a challenge and she was going to rise to it.

Gunfire

Stacey let Rex take her where he wanted to go. That turned out to be past all the stallholders and shops on Higher Market Street and through the alley that led down to the headland overlooking Pen Rocks.

She thought that was where they were heading until Rex took a different path, one that led down toward the coast.

"There's nothing down here, Rex," she pointed out, wondering where the dog was taking her.

Rex didn't bother to argue. He was following a stack of human scents and none of it added up to anything he was happy with.

His human was ahead of him, that was the main thought going around his canine mind. Rex needed to find Albert just so he could be sure the old man was okay. He would have been worried enough under normal circumstances, but coming past the hotel his nose had caught Tanya's scent.

It made him quicken his pace, especially when it became obvious she had gone in the same direction as Albert. Worse yet, Rex considered, Albert's smell was intertwined with another – that of the man whose scent Rex first detected this morning on the clothes of the dead man.

Rex still wasn't sure what it meant, but he suspected his human had been trying to solve the murder all day and was once again up to his neck in trouble.

The sound of gun shots brought his ears up.

Stacey froze. They were almost at the beach and just twenty or so yards from the boat sheds. The sound of gunfire had to compete with the ever-crashing waves and would not be heard by anyone in town, but there was no mistaking what it was.

Rex exploded into action, bursting into a straight out run before the sound of the first shot could fade. His collar snapped from Stacey's grip, jerking painfully against his throat though he never thought to slow down.

There were people ahead of him in one of the boat sheds. He knew which one and could follow the trail as if it were painted on the floor in luminescent colours. The smell of cordite from the bullets made it even easier.

Heading for the only wooden building with light spilling from inside, Rex didn't have to look for a door because it flew open.

Silhouetted in the doorway like a dancer caught in a strobe light, Tanya was there one moment and gone so quickly Rex would have questioned his eyes if his nose didn't already know the truth.

In a snap decision, he altered his course and chased her.

Twenty yards behind him, Stacey was yet to move. Running toward a gunfight was not something she would ever do.

She too saw Tanya burst through the door of the boat shed and vanish into the darkness.

When Cody's face appeared a moment later, framed in light just inside the door, Stacey's heart skipped. Was Rodney here too? Was he alright?

Getting her feet to move, she took a pace and stopped again. Cody had his arm around someone. That someone turned out to be Terry, the pasty shop owner framed in the same piece of light as Cody when the shorter stockier man carried/dragged his friend out of the boat shed to reveal Raven holding Terry up from the other side.

He was clearly injured; not that Stacey could see what was wrong with him. Too scared now to hold back, she started running toward them.

Unaware that she was being pursued by Albert's dog, Tanya reached the water's edge and leapt. Landing two-footed on the deck of Kelly and Liam's boat, the one they were going to escape on once they had the people they needed, she ran for the control room.

The pasty makers had come from nowhere, startling her when they just walked into the boat shed chatting with each other like they were out for a stroll.

She shot the first one in the chest: a perfect kill shot as she intended.

Then her stupid gun jammed, saving the woman who had a wonderful confused/stunned look on her face.

Tanya figured she could dispatch her party crashers just as easily with a knife, but the first victim, Cody, chose that moment to wake up. In fact, Tanya realised as he lashed out with a leg to sweep her feet, he had clearly been awake for some time and had wisely waited for the right moment to launch his attack.

Hitting the floor of the boat shed, a roll took her out of Cody's reach, and she came up with a knife in her right hand.

Cody had one of his own and now facing off against him and Raven both, Tanya had calculated her odds. A glance at Albert garnered a wry smile and a jaunty salute before he turned and ran for a window on the far side of the building.

Recovering from her initial shock, Raven had snatched a heavy iron bar from the floor and was circling, paying no attention to Terry as he clutched at the blood coming from his chest.

Cursing her luck, and knowing Albert Smith was going to slip through her fingers one more time, Tanya ran at Raven. The woman's eyes went wide with surprise, and in that moment of self-doubt, Tanya took the upper hand.

A swipe of the knife, feigning to the left and striking where Raven least expected it, drew a deep cut to her left forearm. Tanya had Cody in pursuit and all Raven had to do was block her path, but she was no fighter. Shunting her bodily, Tanya kicked the door open and used the frame to help her change direction.

In her wake, Raven screamed for Cody to help her. He crashed through the door a second behind Tanya, but she was already gone, swallowed by the darkness and the sound of her flight masked by the waves crashing into the pontoons.

"I think I'm dying," wheezed Terry, looking down at his shirt. It was soaked with blood, the hole in it right in the centre of his chest.

"Where's the old man?" Cody raged, adrenaline pushing his pulse so it hammered in his head.

His question was answered by the roar of a boat engine.

Unable to believe his ears, Cody bellowed, "He's taking my boat!"

Albert was doing no such thing. The moment attention had swung away from him, he'd run to the one window set into the wall behind him. Clambering out hadn't been easy, and he'd lost his grip, knocking the air from his lungs when he tumbled five feet to the hard concrete outside.

Winded, he had to force himself to get up and get away. He'd come to Looe to end the Gastrothief's crimes. Right now all he could think about was survival.

He too heard the boat's engine roar to life and was looking the right way when he saw it take off – a sleek sunseeker style yacht. What he didn't see was Rex.

Chasing Tanya, Rex was just arriving at the end of the pontoon when she threw the throttle all the way to its stop. The boat leapt forward, tearing the mooring cleat from the back of the boat and it was blind luck that Rex managed to land on the deck and not in the churning wake.

Though successful in his aim, Rex was unable to keep his footing and struck his head when he fell. Seeing stars, he blacked out and was lying flat in the deck out of sight when the boat shot off across the water.

Tanya had neither seen nor heard the dog and jumped half out of her skin when she checked her six and found Rex lying on her deck. Her heartrate slowed when the dog didn't get up.

"Knocked yourself out, eh? Let's see how well you can swim."

Confession

"Stacey! You treacherous cow! Who was that woman?" Cody barked as she approached.

Stacey didn't answer his questions. "What the ... What happened to Terry? Did someone shoot him? What the heck is going on?"

Cody pushed by her, carting Terry toward his boat. Upon exiting the boat shed, he was relieved to find his trusty old vessel exactly where he had left it.

"It's none of your business," Raven spat. "Keep your nose out if you know what's good for you."

Unwilling to block their path – it was clear Terry needed immediate medical assistance, Stacey nevertheless kept with them.

"Where's my brother?" she demanded. "What are you all mixed up in?"

Cody dropped Terry to grab Stacey. Twice her weight and considerably stronger, Cody grabbed her around the neck and started to drag her towards his boat.

She fought back, striking his arm and kicking out at him, but her blows were ineffectual and making little difference to the inevitable outcome – Cody was going to put her on his boat.

With a muted cry of pain, Terry sagged into Raven and then collapsed to the ground.

"I can't do it by myself, Cody!" Raven shouted for him to return. "Forget Stacey! Terry needs help!"

Cody spun around still holding Stacey by the back of her neck.

"She knows!"

"Knows what?" Stacey begged to know as she continued to thrash.

From the concrete where she was trying to convince Terry to get up, Raven screamed a response, "She doesn't know anything, Cody! Rodney told her about the engagement, that's all."

Incensed, Cody spat, "That's more than anyone should know. We have to silence her!"

Raven's head and eyes shot around to look up at her boyfriend.

"Is that what happened to Chris? Did you silence him?"

Cody was unrepentant.

"He would have talked. You heard him last night. He said we were going too far. Our plan demands secrecy!"

"What plan?" squealed Stacey, horrified that she was in the grip of a killer. His confession was not lost on her. Nor was the dismissive tone in which he admitted his crime. "What are you mixed up in? Where is Rodney? What have you done with him?"

Cody's attention had been split for too long and failing to pay sufficient attention to Stacey meant he didn't see when she fished a nail file from her pocket. As a stabbing weapon it was never going to do much damage, but plunging it into Cody arm was enough to slacken his grip.

She slipped free and ran, tearing across the concrete and into the dark with Cody on her heels. She heard when he tripped and fell, but didn't slow down. Only when she had covered fifty yards and dared to risk looking over her shoulder did she gasp with relief and ease her pace and stop.

Bathed in light from the boat shed, Cody and Raven were loading Terry onto the boat. They were carrying Terry by his shoulders and feet, his form hanging limp between them.

Stacey could barely believe what was happening. It was all too much. Albert had been right about the woman he had followed earlier; Tanya was a gun-toting killer for hire. However, that wasn't the only thing going on.

She had to call the police.

Taking out her phone, Stacey squealed with fright when a dark shadow crossed her path.

"Oh, lord. Albert, you scared me," she clutched her heart. "Are you all right? Hold on, what are you wearing?"

His bowler hat was missing, and his make up was a mess. The right shoulder of his suit was ripped, the innards hanging out with loose bits of cotton flapping in the breeze.

Albert could see Stacey was unharmed, so he only had one question, "Where's Rex?"

Out to sea

Rex woke up when the cold water hit his skin. Opening his eyes, panic gripped him instantly. He was underwater, as his gasp for air had revealed.

Choking and coughing, he bobbed to the surface in time to see the tail end of the boat heading back to the distant lights of the shore.

He coughed some more; the sea water he'd inhaled refusing to leave him be. Paddling in place and looking around, he had stars above him and darkness in every direction save one. The lights of the town seemed impossibly far away and vanished from view three times a second as the sea bobbed him up and down.

It was a bad situation to be in, he understood that.

His head hurt and he had a slight taste of blood. Shifting his tongue around inside his mouth, he found the source - a loose tooth on the left bottom side of his mouth.

It was the least of his concerns.

With no option, he began paddling for shore.

Ten minutes later, he couldn't be sure, and wanted to tell himself it was just his imagination, but the lights of the town looked to be further away not closer.

The tide was carrying him out to sea and no matter how hard he paddled, he was never going to get back to Looe under his own steam.

Time's Up

Albert's heart ached. According to Stacey, Rex had chased Tanya. The Gastrothief's assassin took the boat Liam and Kelly arrived on, and since Rex hadn't returned or answered when he called, Albert had to assume his dog was on the boat.

There was nothing he could do about that, but what he could do was head off Tanya's colleagues. They were about to grab the winners of the cider competition. They said the announcement was in forty minutes time and that was more than half an hour ago.

He had to find them and follow them. Tanya said she would collect them from the quayside, so unless they changed the plan, which Albert acknowledged they could easily do, he even knew where they were going to be.

He was going to find Kelly and Liam, make sure they had their victims with them, and then, like an avenging angel, he was going to bring the local police down on their heads. It sounded like a long shot … heck it was a long shot, but it was all Albert had and nothing was going to stop him from trying.

Or so he thought.

Convinced Stacey was coming with him as he aimed his feet back toward the town, he stopped when she not only failed to accompany him, but burst into tears.

The waterworks was an unfair tactic, he'd always felt. How is a man supposed to manage a grown woman crying? Oh, he'd developed a thick skin during his years in the police, but now, knowing Stacey probably had cause for concern and had been dragged into his strange and dangerous little world, he couldn't just tell her to snap out of it.

Sucking on his cheek, he reached out what he hoped was a supportive hand and placed it on her shoulder.

"Um, you're worried about Rodney, right?"

He got a response, but it came amid a sob and snot-filled wail that blended the words into an unintelligible mess.

Guessing what she might have intended him to hear, he licked his lips and tried, "Uh-huh. Well, if we assume he is okay, but in need of help, there's no good in staying here. The stakes are far higher than I ever believed and honestly, I don't really know what's happening. What I do know, is that we have one chance to stop them. If the Gastrothief's agents have Rodney, we have one shot at getting him back."

Stacey sucked in a shuddering breath before blurting, "What if they don't have him? What if ... what if Cody and Raven have done something to him? Whatever they are involved in is waaaay bigger than I ever imagined. I mean, I can't go home. Even if I wanted to, I couldn't because Cody thinks I know too much and need to be silenced." She gasped, remembering a key point she had failed to disclose. "Cody killed Chris! He admitted it like he was proud of what he had done. Cody said Chris was going to talk about what they had planned because he didn't agree with it."

"What do they have planned?"

"I have no idea, Albert. He wants to silence me though. He acted like it was something that had to happen. If he'd got me on his boat, I might be dead already." Her face crumpled and she started crying again.

"Look we don't even know if he's seen Rodney today," Albert guessed what was upsetting Stacey and tried to put a less concerning spin on it. "If he comes back for you, that's good. We can catch him too."

Albert pursed his lips, recalling the questions Cody had thrown at him.

"Cody asked what I knew about his operation. It's something to do with the royal engagement and Terry's Pasty Shop."

Stacey wiped her face and took Albert's handkerchief when he offered it.

"Thank you," she sniffed. "Yes, he said as much to me. Said I knew too much about it even though I don't know anything at all."

Cody was a problem. He had to be brought to justice, but not only was it not Albert's job to do so, he had just one shot at clearing his name and he had to act right now.

"I have to stop Liam and Kelly – that's Tanya's friends," he explained, "the ones I saw her with earlier. They are on their way to grab the winners of the cider competition right now. If I'm right, they will be out of Looe for good in less than an hour. Maybe sooner. I was right about the pasty shop being their other target; they knew Cody when they saw him and said they were planning to kidnap Chris Mason and Terry the owner. That's not going to happen, but I think they will cut their losses."

"So what are you saying?"

"That there is nothing we can do about Cody. Unless he is an idiot, his boat is pointed toward the horizon and he's not coming back. I have to stop Tanya and the others. The moment I know where to bring the police, that's precisely what I will do. Then you can tell them about Cody and Terry and me. They will send the coast guard to catch Cody. Or the Royal Navy even. He won't get away but there is nothing either of us can do about him right now."

"You want me to just give him a head start?" Stacey's expression was incredulous. "What if he has got Rodney?"

Albert couldn't think of any other way to put the same point across, and they were running out of time.

Stacey let her shoulders sag. They were staring at each other, and both felt a need to act.

"Listen, um, Albert. I can't go along with this any longer. I'm going to tell the police." Stacey saw disappointment and acceptance in Albert's eyes. "The first officer I see, I'm going straight up to him or her. That Tanya woman shot Terry; I saw the gun in her hand when she ran out of the boat shed. I must report what I know before anyone else gets hurt. I know you want to catch them and clear your name, but what if they get away? You said they were going to kidnap cider makers. What if they do and you can't stop them?"

Albert had no argument, and said, "You should do what you think is right, Stacey, but if the police stop me before I get to Rex, Tanya will kill him. I am certain of it." He refused to consider that she might have already done so. "You have to give me enough time to find him, Stacey."

"I can't promise you that, Albert. I'm sorry."

It was a stalemate.

There being nothing else to say, they started walking again, pushing up the narrow road that led back to town. Loud music started up before they made it back to the Cliff View Hotel, suggesting the evening's entertainment was already underway and unlikely to stop. That meant they had missed the winning cider being announced and were most likely already too late to catch Kelly and Liam.

His tactic for finding them was predicated entirely upon knowing roughly where they would be at a given time. He'd missed his window.

Hurrying onward, past the Cliff View Hotel and through the alley that led them back to Higher Market Street once more, Albert pushed his body harder than it wanted. He knew he would reap the unpleasant rewards later and believed the bruising from today's adventures was going to leave his body set like a rock come the morning.

Emerging onto Higher Market Street, the crowd of people in the town had diminished not one bit. If anything, there were more visitors now that the sun had set and the stalls selling alcohol were doing a roaring trade.

Albert got a few looks, his wrecked living statue outfit drawing several comments, but he barely heard them. His focus was singular: find Kelly and Liam, trail them to Tanya and get Rex back.

There were no cops immediately in sight, a mercy Albert thanked the Lord for.

“I’m going to the beach,” he told Stacey. “Are you coming with me?” Albert could see she was looking for people in uniform, standing on the tips of her toes to see over peoples’ heads. When she didn’t answer straight away, he added, “They will be on the beach or heading to the quayside, Stacey. We can still get them."

She turned toward him.

"I'm sorry, Albert. I know what you want to do, but I can't help you. I waited until we got here, hoping there would be police in sight. There aren't, so I'm going to call them." She had her phone in her hand and when it rang, she almost dropped it.

"It's Rodney!" she scrambled to answer the call when she saw his name on the screen. "Rodney, where are you? Are you okay? What's going on?"

Things Just Get Worse

"I'm sorry, Stacey," sneered Cody. "Rodney can't come to the phone right now. He's too badly hurt."

A faintness crept over her, and she looked for something to take her weight. Albert stepped in close to shore her up.

"Cody," he spoke into the phone. "There is no need for any further bloodshed. Neither one of us knows anything about your … operation," he employed the same word Cody had chosen to use. He had more to say, but was cut off.

"Oh, I wish I could believe you. Unfortunately, I don't. I want you both to come to the quayside. Alone. I see a cop and I'll sail out to sea and ditch Rodney over the side with a lead weight around his feet."

Stacey gasped and had to bend at the waist to stop herself from passing out.

Albert replied for her. "Ok, Cody, we are coming to you. Just don't hurt Rodney."

They both heard the cruelty in Cody's laugh. "It's a bit late for that," he taunted. "I'm afraid Rodney has been a rather naughty boy. He's not dead though. Not yet. But he will be if you don't meet me at the southern tip of the quayside in half an hour. Come alone." The line went dead.

There was no colour in Stacey's face. All around her, happy revellers were eating and drinking and having a wonderful time. They were completely oblivious to the nightmare playing out right next to them.

Tearing her eyes away from her phone, she looked up at Albert's face.

"What do we do? If we go, Cody will kill us. But how can we not go?"

Albert's mind was racing, striving to find a strategy that might still allow them to win. Nothing came to mind; he was hopelessly beaten. Until a solution appeared in the most unexpected of ways.

Gripping Stacey's hand, he tugged her along as he set off.

"The pickpocket, what did you say his name is?"

Stacey blinked and ran the question through her head in case she might have heard it all wrong.

"The ... what?"

"The young lad who stole the lady's purse earlier today. You said you thought he was someone you recognised."

"Yeah, but, I didn't get a very good look at him."

"Well, what was the name if it was the boy you know?"

Unsure why Albert was asking, she nevertheless supplied an answer, "Ricky Brogden."

Albert lifted a hand to his mouth.

"Ricky! Hey, Ricky!"

A hooded youth turned his head their way.

Stacey swore, "Oh, my goodness. It is him. The dirty little beggar."

The kid's eyes widened with panic, and he turned to run. It was too late for that though because Albert was only a couple of yards away when he called the name.

Risking injury if the kid fought back, Albert gripped hold of the hood and yanked it up and then down. Effectively blinding the pickpocket, Albert trod on his right foot and gave the kid a push.

Ricky tumbled to the ground, landing without grace and finding Stacey in his face when he finally shoved his hood back and tried to get up.

"Does your mum know you are out here stealing from people?" she challenged indignantly.

Sitting on the pavement and leaning back to get some space between his face and Stacey's, Ricky shrugged.

"Yeah, how else do you think she pays the bills since dad died?"

His answer took the wind out of her sails, but it was Albert who had the next question.

"How would you like to do a good deed and earn some money. It might even make you famous."

Sleight of Hand

At the beach, the sound booming out of the giant speakers mounted either side of the stage was loud enough to make Albert's teeth hurt. The band on stage was not one Albert had heard of and the tune they were playing was nothing he recognised.

Not that he was listening. His focus was on the helpful event organiser they found. Going by the name Ryan, Stacey knew him much as she seemed to know almost everyone residing or working in Looe and needed only seconds to discover the name of the winning brewers.

Valley Orchard of Wadebridge, a spot on the map on the other side of Cornwall, had bagged first prize for their cider which they fermented inside old whisky barrels.

Albert didn't care about that. He wanted to know where they were.

Pointed in the direction of the promenade, Ryan revealed they had been approached by a pair of reporters with a TV camera. He last saw them heading away from the beach to find a less noisy spot for an interview.

Albert could have asked Ryan to describe them, but he already knew the reporters were Liam and Kelly. It explained their smart clothes and was a typically clever tactic to separate the targets from everyone else. How else would they kidnap people in plain sight of so many witnesses?

The winners were brothers according to Ryan, who was good enough to provide a brief description.

With Ricky in tow, because Stacey was giving him no choice in the matter, all three of them raced back to town.

“They could be anywhere,” Stacey pointed out. “What are we doing this for anyway, Albert? What are we going to do about Cody and my brother?”

“Sleight of hand, my dear. If we can.”

“Sleight of hand?”

They paused at the end of the promenade and peered at the busy streets ahead.

“Yes. To perform what people think of as magic tricks, magician’s employ sleight of hand. It means making the audience look at one hand while you are doing something to confound them with the other.”

“Yes, Albert, I know what sleight of hand is. How the heck does that help us?”

Rather than try to explain, he said, “It doesn’t if we can’t find them, and we are looking in the wrong place. They are not going to be somewhere crowded.”

Stacey spasmed and pointed. “Wait, that’s them. Isn’t it?”

Albert pushed her arm down. She had done it. Looking for two people in a sea of thousands and she had done it.

Kelly and Liam were pushing two wheelchairs and looking every bit like a couple taking their elderly parents out for the evening. Wrapped in blankets against the cool air and with hoods to cover their faces, the winning brewers would not be recognised by anyone.

Liam and Kelly had lured the brothers away and either hit them with stun guns or drugged them somehow. Albert suspected the latter because it would make them compliant and controllable, not unconscious and unpredictable if they came around.

Whichever it was, the Gastrothief's agents were heading back into the town and that suited Albert just fine.

"Okay, kid. You're up."

Ricky smiled in the stupidly overconfident way that only a teenager can achieve.

"Piece of cake."

Albert and Stacey went with him, hanging back ten yards and hoping nothing would go wrong. They were employing a criminal to stop other criminals but at the same time they were sending a teenage boy up against two armed killers. If he botched picking a pocket, Albert didn't want to think what they might do.

There proved to be nothing to worry about, Ricky's accidental and apologetic bump and jostle resulting in Liam's phone changing ownership.

Heading back to Stacey and Albert, he grinned and showed them what he had.

"Stage one," Albert murmured.

Failing Subterfuge

Albert tried to do it himself, but quickly learned that he couldn't even get Liam's phone to open its home screen.

"What do you want to do?" asked Ricky, tutting at the geriatric old man trying to use basic modern technology.

"Send a text message."

"To who?"

"Whom," Albert corrected the young man's English automatically.

"Huh?"

Albert said, "Nevermind. I want to send it to Tanya."

Ricky fiddled with the phone for almost a second.

"What do you want it to say?"

Albert looked at Stacey when he said, "Need a new meeting spot. Police everywhere. Come to southern tip of quayside in ten minutes."

Stacey's eyes bugged from her head as she saw Albert's plan. He was going to put Cody and Tanya in the same place at the same time.

"What if Tanya or someone starts shooting again?" she asked.

Albert shrugged. "I'm kind of counting on it. Nothing will get the police moving faster than a few bullets flying around. You said the quayside is always quiet at night. That's why Cody chose it."

Liam's phone pinged and three faces peered down to read the message.

"Are you smoking something? Kelly just sent me that same message five minutes ago. I'll see you in five, stupid."

"She's not particularly tolerant, is she," observed Stacey.

Albert bit his lip. He'd figured that by changing where the Gastrothief's agents were going to meet, Liam and Kelly would get cut off. He wanted Tanya to arrive in the wrong place right when Cody showed up. It would start a fight and he was going to bring the police down on top of them while praying to God that no one got hurt.

In the mop up afterward, Liam and Kelly would be found with the kidnapped brewers and, Albert hoped, the truth would come out in the wash.

Now it was going to go different to how he imagined and there was nothing he could do to change it.

"What do we do now?" asked Stacey.

"We go to meet Cody."

"I can go then?" asked Ricky, already backing away.

Albert almost said 'Yes' but his cop brain kicked in to alter the words that left his mouth.

"How much was in his wallet?"

"What wallet?" Ricky replied, his lie falling way short of convincing.

Albert held out his hand until Ricky's grumpy face gave in.

Feeling generous though he couldn't explain why, Albert handed the youth Liam's cash. It looked to be about two hundred pounds. The wallet went into Albert's pocket to be examined later.

"Now you can go." Albert let Ricky start moving before shouting after him, "And stop picking pockets!"

Stacey was looking at him when he swivelled his feet around to face her again.

"Is this really going to work, Albert?"

He wanted to say something that would reassure her. But chose to be honest instead.

“Maybe. You want your brother back and he may or may not be on Cody’s boat. I think he probably is. I want Rex back and you say you saw him get onto Tanya’s boat. They are going to arrive at roughly the same time and when they do, they will be too busy with each other to notice the police arriving.”

“When do we call them?”

“Not until both Cody and Tanya show up. If we do it too soon, they will swoop, Cody or Tanya or both will see them and will simply turn their boats around.”

"Can't we explain what is happening and get them into position first or something?"

"How long do you think it will take to explain in a convincing enough manner that they agree to go along with it and not just arrest me on the spot? Bearing in mind that we have just over two minutes until Cody and Tanya are both due to arrive."

Stacey's phone rang, Rodney's name appearing on the screen again. It was an answer to her question and proved Albert's point.

Tapping the green button with a thumb, she said, "Hello?"

"Where are you," demanded Cody. "I said to meet me at the quayside. You have exactly one minute or I'm leaving with your brother, and you can start planning what to say at his funeral."

Terrified all over again, Stacey blurted, "I'm coming! Don't leave. I'm nearly there."

Further Out to Sea

Rex's legs were getting tired. The shore was definitely farther away than it had been, and he was getting cold. Giving up wasn't in his nature, but he was starting to question what would happen when he simply couldn't make his legs continue paddling.

Mostly during the last half an hour, he'd been thinking about Albert. Was he all right? Had he escaped unscathed? It bothered Rex that he might never find out.

It also bothered him that he'd never eaten a T-bone steak, but questioning whether he ought to just stop swimming, the surface of the water churned just ahead of him. When a round head popped out of it a moment later, Rex almost backflipped to get away. Drowning was one thing. Getting eaten by a sea monster was entirely less palatable.

“Dog, what are you doing all the way out here?” asked Gus.

A Sight They'll Never Forget

Cody crouched on the starboard side of his boat, holding onto the mooring point with one hand because he had no intention of tying off. He was going to make Stacey and the old man get on board, force them to tell him what they knew, and then make them both disappear.

If the trail ended with them, and there was nothing on the news to suggest he was being pursued, he would return to Looe.

It was a shame about Terry, but other than Raven, Stacey and the old man, no one knew he'd been killed unless one counted the mad woman who shot him.

Cody still had no idea who the woman with the gun was, but if he ever saw her again … well, let's just say the unlicensed shotgun he kept on his boat had been cleaned and loaded in the last half hour.

Stacey walked into a puddle of light on the quayside, emerging from the darkness between two buildings.

"Where's the old man?" Cody snarled when he didn't appear behind her.

"He's coming," she replied, twisting around to look back into the darkness behind her. "He's in his eighties," she guessed Albert's age, "and he's injured."

Cody barked. "I don't care."

Albert wasn't behind Stacey at all. Thinking in terms of sleight of hand again, he'd taken Church End to emerge forty yards down the street and closer to the beach. If Tanya was coming, he wanted to know first so he could spring the trap.

Peering out to sea, a black shape against a black background became another boat a few seconds later. A sleek yacht, in fact.

Tanya was here.

With a deep breath to steady his nerves, Albert lifted his phone and prepared to dial three nines.

Naturally, that was when his plan unravelled.

"I'll take that," said Liam, jabbing a gun into Albert's spine.

Kelly came at him from his left side, the wheelchair stopping in front of Albert's feet.

"Tanya was right about you. You are tenacious."

"Like a cockroach," Liam added.

They could see Tanya approaching, but they hadn't noticed Cody yet and he hadn't seen them.

Albert waited, a gun in his back and a whisper of a chance that things could still go his way. He wanted Tanya to dock her boat and be stationary, but as usual that didn't go his way either.

Cody shouted at Stacey, demanding to know where Albert was. Until he did, neither Liam not Kelly had even noticed the crouched figure.

Now looking his way, Liam couldn't believe his eyes. Tanya told them about shooting the pasty shop owner and they'd thought they were going to have to explain to the Earl why they had failed to bring him the pasty maker he wanted. Now one of them was right here. Taking his gun from Albert's back, he pushed the old man a yard further out into the quayside to make it easier for Kelly to cover him.

"Won't be a moment," he said jovially, double pumping his eyebrows at his partner.

Cody saw Albert first, the movement catching his eye just as the old man stepped out of the shadows. His first thought was that Stacey had chosen to pull a trick of some kind. Then he saw Liam.

Cody had no idea who the new player was, but he saw the gun in Liam's hand and assumed he was a cop.

His shout drew Raven, who popped her head out from the below decks cabin just in time to see Liam aiming at Cody.

Stacey wanted to bark a warning, but genuinely couldn't figure out who she was supposed to be trying to save.

Liam was twenty yards from her when Raven fired her shotgun. The whump of noise from it caught the ear of Superintendent Charters. She was positioned close to the bridge, some two hundred yards up the river bisecting Looe and knew precisely what the noise was.

The pellets sprayed Liam, peppering him to cause multiple injuries. His gun went off, an impulse reaction to the pain he felt.

Tanya, who had been focused on bringing the boat alongside the quay without hitting anything, was jolted into looking around when the shotgun fired. Consequently, she saw when Raven stepped onto the deck of Cody's boat to make a target of herself.

Drawing her gun, she took careful aim and pulled the trigger.

Stacey's hand flew to her face when she saw Raven drop. It acted as a catalyst to get her moving. Her brother was on Cody's boat, or so she believed, and the only way to know for sure was to get on board and look.

Cody was in the way, but when Tanya's gun barked again and he took off running, Stacey knew she had to risk it all and go for broke.

Liam was on his knees, and largely out of the fight, but managed to squeeze off a shot when he saw a woman running toward the boat where the shot had come from.

Albert had hesitated when the shotgun blast cut Liam down, and any opportunity he might have had to get away vanished in that moment of inaction.

Kelly, grimacing at the turn of events, placed the muzzle of her gun against the back of Albert's neck and told him to, "Get on the boat."

She was going to hand him off to Tanya, get the brewers on board, and if possible, go back for Liam in that order.

The sound of excited barking made her look to her left.

Albert looked too. His brain insisted he was hearing Rex, but he knew that couldn't be right. He didn't know if his dog was on Tanya's boat still, but he was certain Rex couldn't be barking from the middle of the estuary.

The cloud that had been hanging in the sky like a thick blanket, chose that moment to part. In the moonlight that streamed through, the sight of a German Shepherd rising from the waves, borne on the backs of two seals was one that would stay with those who saw it forever.

Kelly shook her head as if that might make the hallucination go away. When it didn't, she ripped the gun away from Albert to point it at the approaching apparition.

Where Albert saw his dog riding on two seals, Kelly's mind believed there was a three-headed sea monster rising from the depths to get her.

Albert thumped into her, sending her shot wild and as the seals touched the quayside to deposit Rex on dry land he knew precisely what to say.

"Sic 'em, boy!"

Cops were converging on the quayside, coming from all over Looe as they attempted to figure out where the shots had come from. They were running and doing so at speed, but all were yet to arrive.

Tanya watched as Albert's dog bounded out of the dark. It had come from nowhere so far as she could make out, and how the heck had it got back to shore anyway?

Tussling with Albert, Kelly could do nothing to stop the dog when it leapt at her.

One moment she was about to floor the old man, the next there was no air in her lungs.

The sound of shouting further up the quayside and the beams of torches swinging around was enough to convince Tanya. She went now, or she didn't get to go at all. Throwing the throttle into reverse, she sent the boat back out into the river.

On the quayside, Kelly saw her ride home leaving.

Rex had winded her, but he was exhausted from his swim and as much as he wanted to, his legs didn't have the spring in them that he needed. Clambering back to his feet, he had to watch as his quarry ran and jumped, grasping the side of Tanya's boat as it left Looe with no intention of ever returning.

Unable to believe all that had just occurred, Albert came down to one knee and opened his arms.

Rex, excited, exhausted, and glad to be alive, wagged his tail and laid his head on his human's shoulder.

Albert wanted to stay like that, but the voices and torch lights were close enough now that he could hear the radios squawking.

"We've got to go, Rex," he levered himself off the ground.

"Albert," hissed Stacey.

He looked around to find her helping her brother to get off Cody's boat. He was moving sluggishly, but he was moving and that was better than Albert had expected.

With no time to waste, Albert nevertheless paused to check on the brewers. Still in their wheelchairs and clearly drugged, their eyes were open and moving. Once satisfied they were not in desperate need of medical attention, Albert had something to say.

"Gents, the police are coming. You should be perfectly safe now. When they come, I want you to pass them this message. I hope you are able to remember it all."

He was about two thirds of the way through when Stacey hissed, "Albert! Come on!"

Finishing as quickly as his lips would allow, Albert clapped the brewers on their shoulders and made good his escape.

They ducked out of sight along Church End only to find police officers heading their way through the crowds of festival attendees.

Stacey grabbed her brother and pushed him into a dark shadow. Instantly they looked like a couple having a canoodle. That wasn't going to work for Albert, but with a zing of inspiration, he lifted his arms into a pose and froze.

The cops ran past the living statue without a second glance.

A New Clue

Safely back inside Stacey's shop, once Stacey had found him a bowl so he could offer Rex water, Albert slumped into a chair.

He was done in. Had he ever had a day like it? A sad smile crossed his face when the answer came back, 'Yes, lots'.

Rodney had been badly beaten and probably needed stitches in his head. Cody had taken him out to sea and once Rodney couldn't escape had laid into him.

Obviously, Stacey pressed him to reveal why and finally, this time, Rodney revealed the truth.

It was nothing Albert would have ever guessed.

Cody, Terry, and the others were anti-royalists. Not the vanilla kind who might boo if Prince William came on TV, but the insane kind who believed they could change society by removing the King, the royal family, and the peerage.

When Terry was asked to supply pasties to the engagement of Prince Marcus and Nora Morley, Cody seized upon the chance to do something despicable.

“Why did you go along with it?” Stacey raged at her little brother. “Do you hate the royal family?”

Rodney shrunk away from her.

"No, I … I dunno. Some of what they said made sense. If the rich elitists weren't taking so much, common folk would have so much more. It stands to reason, don't it?"

"NO!" shouted Stacey.

Albert didn't have the energy to point out the enormous flaws in the statement Rodney had just attempted to make. Instead, he asked, "Would you have willingly murdered members of the royal family."

Rodney looked horrified. "No, not murdered them. Just give them an upset tummy or something. I know that's not what Cody said he wanted to do, but I figured maybe I could … I dunno," he concluded after a moment and fell silent.

Stacey wanted to hit him across the head with something, but pulled him into a hug and held him like that.

The quiet in Stacey's shop gave Albert time to reflect. Tanya and Kelly had escaped. He didn't know what had happened to Liam or whether his wounds were survivable, but unless he was alive and confessing, once again Albert had nothing to show the police.

To have come so close to catching them, so close to clearing his name was infuriating. He could have been on his way home in the morning. What was he supposed to do now?

A single clue: a hotel booking in an email on Baldwin's phone had led him to Cornwall. He'd rolled the dice and got it right, but even though he'd been right here on top of them and had figured out who they were going after, he still hadn't been able to stop them. Or catch them. Or produce one shred of worthwhile evidence.

Remembering Liam's wallet, he retrieved it from his coat pocket. It contained credit and debit cards, all in the fake name Liam had given at the hotel. There were no photographs or receipts, no odd little things a person tucks into the folds along with their cash. In fact, it wasn't until Albert was closing it again that he spotted the corner of something poking out from behind a credit card.

Pinching it between thumb and finger-nail, he slid it free.

It was the stub from a betting slip.

Instantly, it brought to mind the one bet he'd ever placed in his life, the stupid long shot horse he'd wasted thirty quid on in Melton Mowbray. The stub for that was still in his suitcase, being used as a bookmark.

Albert made a mental note to look up if the horse had even finished the race. If he ever made it home that is.

Turning the stub over, he found an address on the reverse side. "Glan-Y-Wern," he read, staring at the postcode. He didn't know where that was, but could tell it was somewhere in Wales.

Maybe he did have a next destination to explore, a new clue to follow.

Eyewitness Reports

Superintendent Charters accepted the cardboard cup of tea with a murmur of thanks aimed loosely at the constable delivering it and wondered what she was going to write in her report.

They had three bodies to add to the one they found on the beach this morning and what had clearly been a multi-weapon shootout in a peaceful fishing village that fell inside her territory. It wasn't so much that she craved a quiet life with no crimes to solve and very little to do, but today had taken things a bit far.

Sergeant Andrews appeared out of the gloom. It was a little after two in the morning and they had all worked far more hours than any thought they would. Soon, she was going to have to start sending people home and calling in a fresh wave of officers. She would stay, that being her responsibility and because she wanted to tell her boss she had exhausted every effort in pursuing a solution to the unexplained deaths.

“Ma’am, the crime scene guys are ready to let the bodies go.”

It hadn't been phrased as a question, but Superintendent Charters recognised it for what it was.

With a nod of her head, she blew across the surface of her tea and took a sip before saying, "Very well. Have they reported anything of interest?"

"Only that the man shot in the chest …" Sergeant Andrews flipped her notebook open when her sleep deprived brain refused to supply the victim's name. "Terrance South was killed at least an hour before the other two victims. Oh, also the calibre of the bullet that killed him appears to be the same as that used on Raven Plumber."

"The autopsies will tell us more," Charters remarked, sipping her tea again. "Anything from any of the cordon points?"

It was a senseless question born of boredom and sore feet. She already knew Albert Smith had not been found. Everyone stationed on the roads in and out of Looe knew to contact her the moment they had him or had a possible sighting of him.

That he might have escaped the town came as no great shock; there were too many ways in and out and that was before one factored in the sea. He could have chosen to walk, picking a cross country route that would take him to the next town by daybreak. There he could climb aboard a bus or train and go anywhere. There were people looking for him, but it appeared the suspected terrorist was also a master of disguise.

She knew this from a pair of eyewitness reports. Eyewitness reports that threw everything she believed into question.

Mike and Thomas Brewer, who were, rather ironically, brewers, were found in the middle of the carnage. Sitting in wheelchairs, the first officers on the scene were confused by their presence and lack of responsiveness.

Paramedics treated them, and in the back of an ambulance the two brothers began to come out of their stupor. They'd been drugged, which was easy to believe, and had a tale to tell that was so ridiculous and fanciful it could only be told by someone with a drug addled mind.

In their eyes, Albert Smith was a hero. Though unable to move or speak at the time, the Brewer brothers' eyes and ears worked just fine so they heard Albert's exchange with their captors and watched him fight them off.

She believed that part or, at least, had no reason to doubt their claims. Albert Smith, whatever he was up to, did not appear to be working with the people doing the shooting. Both brothers were adamant Albert Smith had not produced a firearm of his own.

They said he had an accomplice; a woman they saw him leave with, but if she accepted that, then she had to believe their report that Albert Smith, on top of stepping in to prevent their kidnap, had been engaged in a rescue mission.

A man, as yet unidentified, but in a terrible state, was taken from the boat on which they found two of the bodies. He left with the woman and Albert Smith.

Furthermore, the suspected terrorist chose to stop to check on the health and wellbeing of the two kidnapped brewers at a time when the police were bearing down on him. These were hardly the acts of a hardened criminal thirsting for blood.

Most surprisingly, they had a message from Albert Smith. He named the man who killed Chris Mason as Cody Williams, a citizen of Looe and the owner of the boat on which they found the bodies of Terrance South and Raven Plumber. If Mr Smith was to be believed, Chris Mason's murder was to do with an anti-royalist plot.

The third man was yet to be identified, and though officially it would have to wait for ballistics to confirm, Superintendent Charters was content that the shotgun wounds he died from came at the hands of Raven Plumber.

Albert Smith's message went on to protest his innocence which was not so unusual, and warned that he was going after someone called 'The Gastrothief'.

Superintendent Charters had no idea who or what a gastrothief was. It was something for the morning. Apparently, there was a chief inspector from Kent on his way to talk to her.

The brothers had been sent to hospital and would be kept there overnight. Superintendent Charters hoped to snatch a couple of hours sleep at the station before heading there to question the Brewer brothers in more detail.

Their story held water and corroborated most of what the police had found on the quayside, but there was one element that defied belief. They insisted Albert Smith had been saved from getting shot by a dog that exploded from the water being carried on the backs of two seals.

It was at that point that their story fell apart. A toxicology screen would reveal what drug or drugs they had been given, but whatever it was, Charters already knew it was going to have a hallucinogen in it somewhere.

A second boat, a sleek yacht had been seen by numerous eyewitnesses leaving the quayside. Launches had been sent to find it without producing a result they believed was the right one. The challenge was how many yachts fit that loose description. The only people who had seen it clearly were drugged off their faces.

Charters hadn't given up on that lead yet, but a worthwhile result looked less than likely.

She downed the rest of her tea and set off to make sure her people were keeping warm and getting their jobs done in an expedient manner; no one wanted to be out here longer than necessary.

The End

Author's note:

Hello, Dear Reader,

When I started writing this book, the royal wedding storyline had been ticking along as a thread in my various series for more than a year. I needed to pull Albert and Rex into that storyline, and this was the book in which I intended to do it.

If you are not aware of that to which I am referring, I have a series with a high-end wedding planner. She has been fighting for the right to manage the next royal wedding, that of the fictional youngest son of King Charles.

Of course, King Charles was Prince Charles when I started writing this book. It only took me seven days from start to finish but in that time, Queen Elizabeth passed.

It demanded some minor rewriting of some early chapters which felt wrong in the aftermath of her death.

Though I express staunch anti-royalist views in this book, I wish to clearly state that they are not my views. I served the crown as a member of Her Majesty's armed forces for just shy of twenty-five years.

This book is set in Looe, a seaside resort I have visited many times in my life. There are pictures of me on the beach as a baby and I have taken my own children there. It is on the other side of the country, but that only makes it a four-hour drive. More than a day trip, but great for a short break.

For anyone reading this who hails from Looe or knows the town well, I apologise for the slightly tortured geography I employ. The boat sheds do not exist, but I needed a location that could be accessed on foot yet far enough away from the town that the sound of gunfire would not be heard.

If you are familiar with my Blue Moon series – another one that will feature in the royal wedding storyline – you may have scratched your head upon reading the names Superintendent Charters and Sergeant Andrews. The pair first appeared in Dead Pirates of Cawsand, the fifth book in my Blue Moon series which makes it seventy books ago as this is book number seventy-five.

Heading back to their stomping ground, I chose to resurrect them.

Often in this series, I remark on Albert's inability to work his phone and other modern devices. This draws far more comment from my readers than I had anticipated. Typically, I find myself being lambasted for portraying an elderly person as technologically incapable. Laughably, this trait of Albert's is based on me.

I have a first class bachelor's degree in Technology, but in my early fifties, I struggle to make my phone do half the things it is supposed to. Were it not for my wife, who at the time of writing is still in her thirties, my phone's battery would have gone dead many years ago and that would have been that.

As a time marker, for those who come to read this book many years from now, it is the end of summer 2022. The Queen is currently lying in state in London with her burial set for Monday, September 19th – next Monday. The sky outside is grey and unhappy, but that comes after a long, hot summer so the cooler temperatures are not only welcome, but long overdue.

I need to go back to the start of this book now and begin the editing process. That will take me a couple of days after which I will start to write my next book. Patricia Fisher beckons. She is in Rio where her adventure continues and promises to be just as deadly as ever.

Take care.

Steve Higgs

History of the Dish

The pasty has been a documented part of the British diet since the 13th Century, at this time being devoured by the rich upper classes and royalty. The fillings were varied and rich; venison, beef, lamb and seafood like eels, flavoured with rich gravies and fruits. It wasn't until the 17th and 18th centuries that the pasty was adopted by miners and farm workers in Cornwall as a means for providing themselves with easy, tasty and sustaining meals while they worked. And so the humble Cornish Pasty was born.

The wives of Cornish tin miners would lovingly prepare these all-in-one meals to provide sustenance for their spouses during their gruelling days down the dark, damp mines, working at such depths it wasn't possible for them to surface at lunchtime. A typical pasty is simply a filling of choice sealed within a circle of pastry, one edge crimped into a thick crust. A good pasty could survive being dropped down a mine shaft! The crust served as a means of holding the pasty with dirty hands without contaminating the meal. Arsenic commonly accompanies tin within the ore that they were mining so, to avoid arsenic poisoning in particular, it was an essential part of the pasty.

The traditional recipe for the pasty filling is beef with potato, onion and swede, which when cooked together forms a rich gravy, all sealed in its own packet! As meat was much more expensive in the 17th and 18th centuries, its presence was scarce and so pasties traditionally contained much more vegetable than today. The presence of carrot in a pasty, although common now, was originally the mark of an inferior pasty.

Filling ideas are endless however, and can be as diverse as your taste will take you. There is much debate as to whether the ingredients should be mixed together before they are put in the pasty or lined up on the pastry in a certain order, with pastry partitions. However, there is agreement that the meat should be chopped (not necessarily minced), the vegetables sliced and none should be cooked before they are sealed within the pastry. It is this that makes the Cornish pasty different from other similar foods.

It was such a commonly used method of eating amongst the miners that some mines had stoves down the mine shafts specifically to cook the raw pasties. And this is how the well-known British rhyme "Oggie, Oggie, Oggie" came about. "Oggie" stems from "Hoggan", Cornish for pasty and it was shouted down the mine shaft by the bal-maidens who were cooking the pasties, when they were ready for eating. In reply, the miners would shout "Oi, Oi, Oi!" However, if they were cooked in the mornings, the pastry could keep the fillings warm for 8-10 hours and, when held close to the body, keep the miners warm too.

Recipe

Ingredients

For the pastry

- 500g/1lb 1oz strong bread flour
- 120g/4oz vegetable shortening or suet
- 1 tsp salt
- 25g/1oz margarine or butter
- 175ml/6fl oz cold water
- 1 free-range egg, beaten with a little salt (for glazing)

For the filling

- 350g/12oz good-quality beef skirt, rump steak or braising steak
- 350g/12oz waxy potatoes
- 200g/7oz swede
- 175g/6oz onions
- salt and freshly ground black pepper
- knob of butter or margarine

Method

Method

1. Tip the flour into the bowl and add the shortening, a pinch of salt, the margarine or butter and all of the water.

2. Use a spoon to gently combine the ingredients. Then use your hands to crush everything together, bringing the ingredients together as a fairly dry dough.

3. Turn out the dough onto a clean work surface (there's no need to put flour or oil onto the surface because it's a tight rather than

sticky dough).

4. Knead the dough to combine the ingredients properly. Use the heel of your hand to stretch the dough. Roll it back up into a ball, then turn it, stretch and roll it up again. Repeat this process for about 5-6 minutes. The dough will start to become smooth as the shortening breaks down. If the dough feels grainy, keep working it until it's smooth and glossy. Don't be afraid to be rough – you'll need to use lots of pressure and work the dough vigorously to get the best results.

5. When the dough is smooth, wrap it in cling film and put it in the

fridge to rest for 30–60 minutes.

6. While the dough is resting, peel and cut the potato, swede and onion into cubes about 1cm/½in square. Cut the beef into similar sized chunks. Put all four ingredients into a bowl and mix. Season well with salt and some freshly ground black pepper, then put the filling to one side until the dough is ready.

7. Lightly grease a baking tray with margarine (or butter) and line with baking or silicone paper (not greaseproof).

8. Preheat the oven to 170C (150C fan assisted)/325F/Gas 3.

9. Once the dough has had time to relax, take it out of the fridge. The margarine or butter will have chilled, giving you a tight dough. Divide the dough into four equal-sized pieces. Shape each piece into a ball and use a rolling pin to roll each ball into a disc roughly 25cm/10in wide (roughly the same size as a dinner plate).

10. Spoon a quarter of the filling onto each disc. Spread the filling on one half of the disc, leaving the other half clear. Put a knob of butter or margarine on top of the filling.

11. Carefully fold the pastry over, join the edges and push with your fingers to seal. Crimp the edge to

make sure the filling is held inside – either by using a fork, or by making small twists along the sealed edge. Traditionally Cornish pasties have around 20 crimps. When you've crimped along the edge, fold the end corners underneath.

12. Put the pasties onto the baking tray and brush the top of each pasty with the egg and salt mixture. Bake on the middle shelf of the oven for about 45 minutes or until the pasties are golden-brown. If your pasties aren't browning, increase the oven temperature by 10C/25F for the last 10 minutes of cooking time.

What's next for Rex and Albert?

THE GASTROTHIEF

Every journey might start with a single step, but where does it end?

Albert Smith and his faithful dog, Rex Harrison, have been on the road for far longer than they ever expected, but they can't go home yet.

Not until they solve one final case.

Free Books and More

Want to see what else I have written? Go to my website.

https://stevehiggsbooks.com/

Or sign up to my newsletter where you will get sneak peaks, exclusive give-aways, behind the scenes content, and more. Plus, you'll be notified of Fan Pricing events when they occur and get exclusive offers from other authors because all UF writers are automatically friends.

Copy the link carefully into your web browser.

https://stevehiggsbooks.com/newsletter/

Prefer social media? Join my thriving Facebook community.

Want to join the inner circle where you can keep up to date with everything? This is a free group on Facebook where you can hang out with likeminded individuals and enjoy discussing my books. There is cake too (but only if you bring it).

https://www.facebook.com/groups/1151907108277718

56. About the Author

At school, the author was mostly disinterested in every subject except creative writing, for which, at age ten, he won his first award. However, calling it his first award suggests that there have been more, which there have not. Accolades may come but, in the meantime, he is having a ball writing mystery stories and crime thrillers and claims to have more than a hundred books forming an unruly queue in his head as they clamour to get out. He lives in the south-east corner of England with a duo of lazy sausage dogs. Surrounded by rolling hills, brooding castles, and vineyards, he doubts he will ever leave, the beer is just too good.

Milton Keynes UK
Ingram Content Group UK Ltd.
UKHW011947140923
428719UK00002B/22

9 781915 757999